"Oh, Ted," she gasped, *"a wolf!"*

THE
VALDMERE MYSTERY

or THE ATOMIC RAY

By MILTON RICHARDS

WILDSIDE PRESS

THE VALDMERE MYSTERY

THE VALDMERE MYSTERY

CHAPTER I.

AT BROWNSVILLE.

It was the largest influx of people that Browns‚ ville had ever known. From all parts of the world, thousands were flocking into the little western town to be on hand for the great event of tomorrow, to view with their own eyes what promised to be—in the language of the press—"the most unusual and far-reaching scientific demonstration of modern times." Professor Valdmere, America's most distinguished scientist, had invited the public to come here and witness the wonders of his newly discovered Atomic Ray.

Professor Valdmere's house, laboratory and workshops had been built just outside the town. Beyond his estate the land sloped away toward a purple chain of hills, known as Granite Ridge. Except where the town encroached, every side of the square, enclosed field, belonging to Valdmere, and

3

in which he had caused to be constructed these queer-looking buildings of brick and stone, was bordered by a prairie as virgin and untouched as in the days of the pioneers. The estate itself was not large, consisting of scarcely more than twenty acres. It was surrounded on all sides by a ten-foot-high woven wire fence, which was known to be electrified. There were guards, too, inside the fence, making their rounds day and night, much after the manner of sentries in the army. The inference was that Valdmere purposed to take no chances. The secret of workshop and laboratory was to be guarded and kept. The public would see nothing except what Professor Valdmere wanted them to see, hear nothing except what he cared to tell them.

It was the newspapers that had brought the crowds. For weeks now they had been publishing interesting and almost unbelievable accounts of the newly discovered Atomic Ray. The nation and the world at large were stirred by these strange stories, but it was not until a few days ago that the interest had reached its present high peak. This had come about as a result of the publication of the following short article in every newspaper of any importance from Los Angeles to New York and from Duluth to New Orleans:

"Professor Conrad Charles Valdmere, noted

American scientist, now temporarily residing in Brownsville in western Montana, at ten o'clock Wednesday morning issued the following statement to the Associated Press: 'I am now prepared to give a public demonstration of the Atomic Ray. The first demonstration will take place near my estate at Brownsville on Monday morning, June 24th, at ten o'clock. A second demonstration will take place at four o'clock and on the following Wednesday, June 26th, at two o'clock. Scientists, representatives of the press and the public at large are cordially invited to be present.' "

There were two boys residing several hundred miles east of Brownsville who were neither scientists nor representatives of the press but who read the announcement and decided to go. They were Ted Winters and Philo Birch, chums and fellow workers at the Northern Airplane Corporation, Minneapolis. Both were interested in the achievements of the great Valdmere. They had read books concerning the man and had been fired by an ambition to learn more of the particular branch of scientific work in which he excelled. Shortly after the publication of the inventor's invitation, they had pooled their resources, secured a week's leave from Mr. Cable, superintendent at the plant and had set out on their momentous journey.

Their arrival at Brownsville came on the evening of the second day. They were set down, so to speak, in the middle of a prairie that the so-called West begins. It looked a good deal more like the real frontier than anything that they had yet clapped their eyes upon. The country smacked of cattle herds, cowboys and six guns, but as yet they had seen nothing much else than the broad sweep of a seemingly untenanted range.

Brownsville proved disappointing, too, but the boys found plenty to absorb their attention just outside the village at the estate of the inventor. They walked out that first night just at sunset, at the hour silence had settled over the prairie and the world was touched with dazzling radiance. They paused near the estate, regarding it with curious eyes: The high fence with the watchmen inside, the half dozen low buildings constructed of stone and cement.

"Valdmere has quite a place here," Ted remarked, advancing close to the fence, his gaze fixed steadily on the view outspread before him. "The stone building off to the right must be his house. That long rambling structure must be his workshop. But what are the other buildings?"

Philo pursed his lips, scowling lightly. He seemed deeply absorbed as was his chum. His right hand rested for a moment on Ted's arm.

"Couldn't possibly imagine. I'd give half the money I own if I could go through and inspect everything. Do you suppose, Ted, that that will be permitted?"

The other laughed. "Out of the question I'm afraid, Philo. Just picture the mob that has gathered here in Brownsville, running riot over the place. Then, too, you must remember that there must be scores of people who would not be satisfied with a casual inspection of the workshops and laboratories. They would go to any lengths to acquire the professor's formulas and secrets."

"I never thought about that," said Philo, "but I can see now that you're right. It would never do. No doubt Valdmere has enemies, too, who might attempt to destroy or tamper with things."

Ted nodded. "Surest thing, Philo. Else why would he have gone to the trouble to put this huge fence and hire so many guards? Absolute secrecy is necessary. Very frequently Valdmere is engaged in experiments for the United States Government. He has perfected many war devices for the Army and Navy. Not so long ago I read in the *Journal of Scientific Research* about his new aerial torpedo."

Ted and Philo turned away from the fence presently and began to retrace their steps toward the hotel in the center of the town. The streets were lined with people, most of them coming out for their first glimpse of the professor's estate. Among them they discerned a small party of Japanese, crafty-looking little men, who walked along attired in panamas, soft shirts and flannels, chattering in their own language.

At sight of them, Philo nudged his friend in the side.

"Great Scott, Ted! What do you think about that? Wonder what motive is bringing them here?"

Ted grinned amusedly. "Of course you'd suspect something underhanded, Philo, but I think you can set your mind at rest. If anyone should ask you, we're quite a cosmopolitan crowd. Nearly every nation is represented. There are Englishmen, Russians, Frenchmen, Italians, Germans and heaven knows what not. Their presence here merely goes to show how important the world at large considers the forthcoming demonstration. In his particular field, Valdmere is without a peer."

Philo drew in his breath sharply. "Gee whiz, Ted, I can hardly wait until tomorrow. I'm glad that we happened to live so close to where Valdmere is working this summer, or we never would have been given the opportunity to come. What is this Atomic Ray?"

Ted shook his head. "I guess nobody knows except Valdmere himself But as I understand it, Atomic Ray, the newspapers say, affords both heat, light and power. It can be made or generated at a very low cost. It is said that it will solve heating, lighting and motive power for all time to come. If it proves to be everything that Valdmere says it is, we are entering upon a new age of industrial development. It will be the greatest invention, or I should say discovery, of all time."

"The Atomic Ray!" mused Philo. "From the name, one would surmise that this ray was made out of atoms."

"That's it exactly. A certain combination of elements comprising an atom. An atom you know, Philo, is the most common thing in the world. Everything is composed of atoms, the water you drink, the food you eat, the fuel you burn, yes, the air you breathe. Upon atomic structure life itself is built. Now atoms are composed of various elements and combinations of elements. I do not quite understand it myself, but from what I have read, it appears that it is possible to separate elements in an atom and put them together again in new combinations."

"But why should anyone bother with it?" asked Philo. "Even when new combinations are made, what advantage is it to the experimenter?"

"I'm afraid you don't understand," said Ted a little petulently. "This ray that Professor Valdmere has perfected is derived from power lurking in atoms. That is the reason it is called an atomic ray."

"I suppose," said Philo brightly, "that Professor Valdmere has gone to a good deal of trouble to find these atoms that possess the necessary energy with which to generate his Atomic Ray."

Ted snorted. "Come, come, Philo. You're talking nonsense. Snap out of it. Get this clearly in mind: Every atom possesses untold electrical energy. There is enough energy in the atoms to be found in a glass of water to blow a city the size of New York into Kingdom Come."

Philo stopped dead in his tracks, glaring at his friend.

"Bunk!" he sputtered angrily. "You're trying to string me now."

"No, it isn't bunk," protested Ted, "and I'm not trying to string you either. If you'd spend a little more of your time reading instead of fooling around making useless electrical devices, you'd know more about it."

"Bunk!" croaked Philo again. "I don't believe it."

Ted's face flushed and he seemed to be on the point of losing his temper.

"Tomorrow, after you have seen a few of Professor Valdmere's experiments, I dare say you'll change your tune."

"I hope so," retorted the skeptical Philo. "I don't doubt for one minute that Professor Valdmere is a great man and has accomplished some wonderful things, but it must be proved to me that one can take an ordinary glass of water, as you have intimated, and make a few passes over it and unleash the tremendous energy that you have spoken of."

"I didn't say that he did that," sniffed Ted. "What I meant was that the potential power is there."

"Bunk!" said Philo for the third time.

"Bunk yourself!" snapped Ted, come to the limit of his patience.

CHAPTER II.

A JOURNALIST

IN the crowded lobby of the Grand Majestic Hotel, a few minutes later, Ted discerned a group of men he presumed to be representatives of the press. He was studying them casually when some-one touched him on the shoulder. Ted swung about and looked into the smiling face of the hotel clerk.

"Mr. Winters and Mr. Birch, aren't you, who registered here this evening taking room sixteen? I wonder if you would confer a favor upon the management?"

"Why, yes," smiled Ted. "What is it?"

"There's a very serious problem here in providing rooming accommodation for all the people who have come to Brownsville. We had no idea there would be so many. The town is overrun. Would you gentlemen object to our putting two or three cots in your room. Though it may be somewhat un-pleasant, it will cut your hotel expenses considerably."

For a time Ted did not answer. This silence on

the young man's part was translated into meaning a refusal.

"Of course, if you object——" began the clerk

"No, it isn't that," Ted hastened to reassure him. "I have really no objection if it's all right with my friend here."

"It's all right with me," grumbled Philo. "I suppose there's no help for it. I hate to think of people walking around all night without a place to sleep."

The clerk thanked them and hurried away. Ted and Philo pushed their way over toward the corner occupied by the representatives of the press. A tall imposing-looking fellow, possessing keen eyes and a self confident manner, was speaking in an earnest voice to the others and, apparently, was being listened to with a good deal of interest.

"I came down here shortly after Valdmere did," the man was saying. "My paper is pretty keen on this scientific stuff. We've been watching the old wizard closely. And all the time I've been here I've killed a story a day. Stuff I couldn't publish. In some ways my paper is too conservative. It would have been duck soup for some of you fellows on the Yellow Press."

A big fellow, who wore spectacles and smoked a cigarette that had burned down to his fingers, protested mildly.

"That's nonsense. If the story had been here you wouldn't have hesitated about taking it. How come that Brandt of the Associated Press didn't stumble upon some of this sensational copy? He's been here almost as long as you have."

"He has not," flatly contradicted the first speaker. "Been here—yes. A few flying trips up from St. Louis. Never stayed more than an hour or two. Naturally he couldn't get a line on some of the things that came under my observation."

"Haugh!" sniffed the big man suddenly burning his fingers and dropping his cigarette to the floor. "Perhaps you'd be accommodating enough to pass some of this dope along. My worthless sheet hasn't any scruples about publishing anything."

The first speaker laughingly shook his head.

"Not on your life, brother."

A thin little man with a short mustache and a determined mouth, unexpectedly broke into the discussion. He turned sharply upon the representative of the conservative journal.

"Now that you've let the cat out of the bag, Bigelow, I'm afraid you'll have to 'fess up. You won't get any peace until you do."

"No," said Bigelow flatly.

"In that case," the little man's voice was tinctured with deep sarcasm, "why all this chattering? Why make an ass of yourself before this distinguished body of the Fourth Estate?"

Bigelow interrupted his tormentor. "Oh dry up. You fellows have been wondering what I have been leading up to. Well, it's this. You can expect trouble before this thing is over. Mark my words, all you fellows who are so cock-sure I've been talking for effect. Just make a mental note of that and when it's all over, I'll give you the merry ha-ha."

"Trouble!" shouted a chorus of voices. "What sort of trouble?"

"I'm not telling you."

The newspaper group lapsed into a thoughtful silence that continued for several minutes. Then a deep voice proclaimed:

"I think I know what's on Bigelow's mind. He's hinting at a conspiracy. The big interests who are going to receive their death blow with the perfection of the Atomic Ray are coming up here to throw a monkey wrench into the professor's machinery. Isn't that true, Bigelow?"

"That's a wild guess," retorted Bigelow, fixing the other with an unfriendly stare. "No use trying to pump me. You fellows ought to be thankful that I've given you a lead without worrying me to death. If you'll excuse me, gentlemen, I think I'll be turning in."

"Good-night, old man. Thanks for the tip,"

mockingly called out one of the party as Bigelow
strode heavily away. Then to the others: "Fat,
self-important Dodo, isn't he?"

"I'm not so sure that he really isn't sincere in
this," responded the little man with the bristling
mustache. "My own personal opinion is that there
will be trouble. But if there is, I'll blame Valdmere himself."

"Why?" demanded several voices.

"Valdmere's one great weakness is his over-ween-
ing vanity. He likes to hear the plaudits of the
crowd. This little drama he's staging up here is
wholly unnecessary. More like a public stunt than
anything else I can think of. If the conceited old
fool puts his head in a noose, it's his own funeral."

Both Ted and Philo gasped. It was the first time
they had heard anyone speak disparagingly of
America's greatest scientist. A hot wave of color
swept up into the former's cheeks.

"I don't think I'd ever like that newspaper man,"
he whispered in Philo's ear.

"Nor me either," sputtered Philo. "Come on,
Ted, let's turn in. These reporters are talking a lot
of nonsense anyway."

Ted nodded his agreement and they turned,
pushed their way over to the desk, secured the key
for their room and made their way up the stairs.
To their surprise, even the halls on the second floor

was filled with people. When they entered their room and switched on the light, they saw that cots had already been placed side by side at one end of the room. While they were undressing, Philo suddenly paused and addressed his chum.

"Ted," he inquired thoughtfully, "do you really suppose there's going to be trouble tomorrow? What do you think Mr. Bigelow was hinting at?"

"Don't know," answered Ted sleepily, "but I guess its nothing to worry about."

"Did you hear what one of them said about the big interests sending representatives here to spoil everything? And why did he say that the Atomic Ray would be a death blow to certain of those big interests?"

Ted removed his tie and sat there, apparently studying his own likeness in the mirror.

"That's all plain enough," he confided to his chum. "If the Atomic Ray proves practicable, it will call for an industrial readjustment. I mean by that, Philo, that certain things that are commodities now will cease to be commodities. You can see for yourself that if the Atomic Ray can furnish cheap power to drive airplanes and automobiles, there won't be any further use for gasoline. If this Atomic Ray can furnish cheap heating for buildings, there won't be any further use for coal. The guns and munitions of the armies and navies will become

worthless, too, because the Atomic Ray will be a
more terribly destructive force than anything heretofore dreamed of."

Philo pursed his lips and regarded the black tips
of his shoes.

"I'll admit that things look bad for those indus-
tries," he mused.

"Yes," replied Ted, "but it can probably be
worked out in a way that will be fair to everyone."

"I hope so," sighed Philo.

"So do I," said Ted.

Then both boys started as the door opened. Two
men walked into the room. At sight of them, Ted's
heart gave a quick flop of apprehension. There
was something about the appearance of the two new-
comers that tended to cause him uneasiness and
alarm.

Their faces were sinister and unfriendly. They
glowered at the boys as they closed the door behind
them, then one of them spoke in a language which
neither Ted nor Philo could understand.

CHAPTER III.

A STARTLING REVELATION.

THE boys were up at dawn the following morning—a bright cheerful dawn that promised fair weather for Professor Valdmere's demonstration. Ted, first to arise, hurried to the window and looked out. Beyond the outskirts of the town, as far as eye could reach, the prairie scintilated and sparkled with the early morning dew. Very plainly he could make out Valdmere's place, the set of low, rambling buildings, the high fence and even the guards themselves who appeared like dark specks limmed against the background of the little village of buildings near the center of the estate. Ted turned to Philo.

"Everything looks promising," he chirped. "A beautiful day. What time is it?"

Before answering, his friend glanced at the dial of his wrist watch.

"Twenty minutes past six. That's early but we seem to be the last to rise." He paused, motioned to the row of empty cots. "Wonder what time they got up? Perhaps they were wiser than we are and anticipated that the dining-room would be crowded. What do you think of those foreign-looking room-mates of ours?"

Ted scowled lightly. "Tough looking customers, aren't they? One almost hesitates to sleep in the same room with them. After they went to bed last night they lay for a long time jabbering to each other in that strange language. They're Russians I think."

"Bolshevicks!" grimaced Philo.

"No, I wouldn't say that. All Russians aren't Bolshevicks, you know. But whatever they are, their appearance surely is not very prepossessing."

A few minutes later, when the boys descended to the dining room, they found every table occupied and a long line near the door awaiting their turn. Philo grinned at his chum.

"Just what I suspected, Ted, but I have an idea. If we wait here it may be eight o'clock before we have a chance to get our breakfast. Let's go outside and see if any of the stores are open. If they are, we can buy cookies and fruit and proceed directly out to Valdmere's place. We may be too late for an early breakfast, but we won't be crowded out of the first place in the line for Valdmere's demonstration."

"That's a go," said Ted, following his friend to

the door. "I'm willing to miss breakfast altogether
if we can do that."

The first two stores they went to were still locked,
but at the third place they met a clerk just opening
the front door. In a few minutes they had secured
their purchases. On the way out to the professor's
estate, Ted observed:

"We aren't the only ones imbued with the big
idea. See the crowd ahead of us down the street."

If those people have had their breakfasts already,
they must have been awake all night. Do you suppose there are any of our roommates in that party?"

"I shouldn't wonder."

At the next street intersection they were crossing
over to the opposite side when a big car, swinging
along toward them, unexpectedly put on its brakes
and slowed down to a full stop. There was only
one person in the automobile, the driver herself, a
young girl in her early teens. She called to them
softly. Surprised, the two boys swung on their
heels and came back.

"Can you tell me the right road to Langdon
Prairie?" trembled the young driver. "I—I—I'm
a stranger here and am not acquainted with the
roads."

The young lady appeared to be deeply agitated.
Her face was white and, in spite of her brave effort
to appear composed, her lips trembled. She was a

very pretty girl and both Ted and Philo felt sorry
for her.

"We're strangers, too," Ted was the first to speak.
"Just came here yesterday to see Professor Valdmere's demonstration. But I can tell you what to
do. Right at the corner, when you reach the main
street, you'll find a grocery store open. The clerk
there will be able to tell you."

"The store on the south side of the street," ap-
pended Philo.

The girl thanked them, started to take a firmer
hold on the wheel, hesitated and with her cheeks
deathly white, suddenly raised her hands to her head
and slumped back helplessly. For a moment, the
two boys stood like wooden statues.

"Why—why, she's fainted!" exclaimed Philo.

Ted was the first to act. Swinging open the car
door, he reached over and assisted the unconscious
young lady to a more recumbent and restful position
in the front seat. Then he switched off the motor.

"Run over to that house," he directed Philo, "and
see if you can get some water. Hurry!"

Inexperienced in matters of this sort, Ted could
almost believe that the driver was dead. Her face
was ghastly. As far as he could see, she did not
breathe at all. It seemed like a very long time before his chum returned. But when he did, they
bathed her face and presently a faint wave of color

ebbed back into her cheeks. Ted continued to apply
the cold cloth to her head.

"We'd better carry her over to the house," suggested Philo, greatly perturbed. "She's in no condition to drive this car. Besides, people are coming
and it won't be long before a crowd will collect."

It seemed a wise procedure. They had raised her
up to a more erect position and were preparing to
lift her from the car when she gave a queer, fluttering little gasp and her eyes opened. For a brief period
she stared at the two young men a little fearfully.

"Oh!" she gasped.

"I'm sorry, Miss, but you fainted," Ted informed
her. "You remember you stopped here to inquire
the way to Langdon Prairie. You mustn't be afraid.
My friend and I will help you into the house. There
is a woman there and you can lie down and in a few
minutes you will feel better."

The girl thrust away Ted's supporting arms, at
the same time steadying herself by getting a firm
hold on the wheel. To the surprise of both Ted and
Philo she drew back away from them as if in terror.

"No, no, no! I mustn't do that. I'm in a great
hurry. I must get to Langdon Prairie just as quickly
as I can."

"You're in no condition to drive to Langdon
Prairie," said Ted firmly.

"But I must," she faltered.

"Then you'd better get someone to drive the car," Philo suggested. "If—if you don't mind, Miss, we could take you down as far as the corner store and see if we could get someone."

"I tell you I haven't time. I'm not acquainted here. If one of you young men will consent to drive me, I'll pay you handsomely."

Now, as a matter of fact, neither Ted nor Philo wished to go to Langdon Prairie. They had no idea how far away it was and they were afraid that by proceeding there they might return too late to witness the professor's demonstration. And yet duty is duty—and there were certain obligations one cannot reasonably neglect. They looked at each other, lips pursed.

"I'll take you," stated Ted finally.

"No," objected Philo, turning upon the girl, "you see, he's more interested than I am in Professor Valdmere's demonstration, and I wouldn't for the world have him miss it."

"That's all right," said Ted, trying to make light of the matter. "Thanks, Philo. You'd better stay."

Philo shook his head stubbornly and went around to the opposite side of the car and swung open the door.

"If you'll slide over, Miss, I'll take the wheel. Good-bye, Ted. Perhaps I'll be back in time anyway."

The motor had begun to purr softly, when, to
Philo's surprise, the rear door opened and Ted
jumped in. Then that young man's voice, firm with
decision:

"Drive on, Philo. If you're going to miss it,
I am too."

The girl started to say something but Ted silenced
her.

"Professor Valdmere is giving another demonstration Wednesday, so it doesn't matter. We're
only too glad to be of service to you. Stop at that
store, Philo," he instructed, "and I'll inquire about
the road. It will only take a minute."

In this Ted was right. A few moments later,
in answer to his inquiry, the clerk willingly pointed
out the way.

"Turn down Main Street," he instructed, "and
keep right on going. You can't miss it. Just ten
miles."

"Thanks," said Ted, bolting for the door.

Soon afterward, entering the car he imparted the
information to his chum. They glided down along
the main street and out into the open country. Big
drops of dew still blinked and twinkled in the grass.
The perfumed breath of grass and prairie flowers
came to him. Philo stepped on the accelerator. A
wind of their own making whipped up around them.
A cloud of dust streamed away behind. For a long

time no one spoke. Then, his voice trumpeting above the roar of the car, Ted leaned over to the girl.

"Is Langdon Prairie a town?" he shouted.

"I don't know," answered the girl.

"Haven't you ever been there?"

"No."

Ted could not help but think that it was all very mysterious. The girl acted very strangly, he thought. "Whom do you wish to see in Langdon Prairie?" he asked curiously.

For a time there came no answer to this. Then the girl half turned in her seat and, reaching back with her left hand, gave Ted a small slip of paper that looked as if it had been torn from the back of an old envelope. In the center of the sheet, roughly scrawled, were three words:

"Langdon Prairie. Dad."

Still holding the bit of paper in his hand, Ted's brow knit together and he looked up quickly at the girl. An inexplicable feeling had swept through him. On the paper were specks of blood.

"My dad is in trouble," sobbed the girl, "and he wrote that knowing that I would come to him. I found the note lying on the floor in his office. Oh, it is terrible," she choked, suddenly covering her eyes with her arm, her body shaking.

"Who is your father?" he asked.

The answer was so startling that even Philo was visibly affected and the car nearly swerved from the road.

"Professor Valdmere!"

CHAPTER IV.

TED MAKES A DISCOVERY.

THE boys could scarcely believe their ears. The sudden revelation of the mysterious young lady in the front seat that she was the daughter of the famous Professor Valdmere and that he, her father, had unexpectedly disappeared, had so dazed and startled both of them that, for a time, neither seemed capable of speech. They sat with lips pursed and eyes slightly staring as she continued:

"I can't describe the feeling, but I awoke this morning sensing that something was wrong. I hadn't slept well either. Usually I rise at seven, but it was just five o'clock by my watch when I slipped out of bed and began to dress. Even then I was trembling, somehow vaguely troubled. Thoughts about Dad were uppermost in my mind. Something kept telling me that he was in some sort of difficulty and wanted to see me. It was a dreadful obsession, increasing with each passing moment. I couldn't get out into the hall quickly enough and make my way to his room. Of course, he wasn't there—I

was aware of that even before I went in, so strong
was that feeling."

"You must have been terribly alarmed," Ted cut
in.

"I was," nodded the girl, "especially when I found
that he wasn't there and that his bed hadn't been
disturbed at all. It is not an uncommon occurrence
for Dad to work all night, so I tried to make myself
believe that he was in his laboratory or shop somewhere."

She paused, her breath catching. The car continued
to thunder along the country road. Ted leaned
forward still farther to catch her next words.

"But he was at neither place. They were just
changing guards as I made my way back toward the
house and asked them if they knew where my father
was. But they told me they hadn't seen him. Then
I went to the office, that strange obsession still
upon me. The minute I opened the door, I could
see that my worst fears were not without foundation. A chair had been overturned and father's steel
safe, built in the wall, had been blown open. I
became suddenly so weak and sick that I had to sit
down. Someone had taken father's precious papers
and had probably murdered him. For a time, I was
so desperate that I just sat there not knowing what
to do."

"I'm not sure how long I was there—perhaps ten

or fifteen minutes. I became stronger after a time
and got up and walked over to the wall safe and
looked inside. Papers were strewn all over the floor
and, almost automatically, I stooped and commenced
to pick them up. The last thing I found was that
scrap of paper."

Again Miss Valdmere paused, putting one hand
to her head.

"Why didn't you go to the guards just as soon
as you found the paper and tell them you believed
that robbery and violence had taken place and ask
them to help you?"

"I thought of that, but I didn't trust the guards.
The way father has our place guarded, there is no
possible chance of anyone entering or leaving without the knowledge of the sentries. But someone did
enter and leave and it must have been with the
guard's connivance or, at least, with their knowledge. Do you blame me for not trusting them?"

Ted scratched his head. "I don't know as I blame
you. But didn't you have any friends you could
have telephoned?"

She shook her head. "It may seem strange to you,
but I don't know a soul in Brownsville. And, as I
told you before, I arrived here for the first time just
a few days ago. Originally we lived in Cincinnati,
but Dad decided that he could pursue his investiga-
tions more secretly in a remote, out-of-the-way place

like this. All the buildings on our estate were completed only last fall and father has resided here only a short time himself. I've been attending school in the East. The summer vacation has just commenced. So you can readily see that I did not know where to turn or what to do."

"And because the note said Langdon Prairie, you suspected that your father had been taken there."

"Yes," admitted Miss Valdmere, "I thought it might be possible."

Ted's thoughts were leaping hither and yon, a hundred conjectures in his mind. However, one thing stood out very clearly—the greatest puzzle of all: How did Professor Valdmere know that his assailants intended to take him to Langdon Prairie? He voiced the thought.

"He couldn't read their minds, you know," Ted concluded.

Miss Veldmere looked at Ted, her expression one of deep concern.

"It does seem queer, doesn't it? But you may depend upon it, Langdon Prairie has something to do with Dad's disappearance. Either he surmised he would be taken there or—or he overheard one of his assailants say so."

Ted doubted if her last conjecture were correct, and also, flashing across his mind, had come the

suspicion that the note which the girl still held in her
hand might not be Professor Valdmere's at all.

"Don't you suppose, Miss Valdmere, that someone
besides your father might have written that note
in an effort to confuse you? Can you positively
identify the hand writing?"

The young lady's deep, blue eyes shadowed.

"No, not positively. But this looks like Father's
writing if it had been done hurriedly. You can see
for yourself," she held it up where it fluttered in the
wind, "that it is almost a hopeless scrawl. If Father
wrote it, he was evidently in a desperate hurry or it
might have been written under very unusual circumstances."

"What do you mean by that?" asked Ted.

"Father might have been tied to something and
might not have had the full use of his arms."

"But wouldn't the men who tied him there have
been very apt to see him do it?"

"Unless they were occupied with other matters.
You see, the office safe was blown open and rifled
and they might have been so busily occupied that
my father had his opportunity."

"Town ahead," suddenly sang out Philo's voice.
"Must be Langdon Prairie."

A short time later they slowed down as they
entered the outskirts of the village. They passed
several other automobiles, then a farmer driving

a team of horses hitched to a lumber wagon and, presently came to a single business street cut straight as a die from one end of the town to the other. Philo drove in to the curb and shut off the motor. The three young people looked at each other inquiringly.

"I don't know just exactly what to do first," Miss Valdmere turned to Ted. "I think, perhaps, it would be advisable not to notify the police just yet. What do you think, Mr.—er——" she paused flushing.

"My name is Winters—Ted Winters, and my friend's is Philo Birch," Ted assisted her. "Yes, Miss Valdmere, I quite agree with you that there would be nothing gained by calling in the assistance of the local police. You can describe your father and ask if a person answering that description has been seen here."

Philo objected. "I don't agree with you. I think we ought to notify the police. They're better ac-quainted here than we are and will have better means of finding out if your dad has been here."

Thinking it over, Ted was about to assent, when a person passing along the street suddenly drew his attention. He popped up, seizing Philo's shoulders in a grip that must have hurt.

"Look!" he whispered hoarsely. "Look, Philo! One of the men that slept in our room last night."

"Cra—cracky!" stammered Philo. "Wha-what do

you suppose he's doing here? Why, Ted," he stared almost increduously, "what are you doing?"

Ted leaped out of the car, his face determinedly set, his eyes shining.

"Listen," he commanded. "I'll meet you here a little later. Philo, will you and Miss Valdmere make inquiries in the meantime? I'm going to follow him. His presence here looks suspicious. It may have something to do with Professor Valdmere's disappearance."

Turning quickly, he leaped to the curb, hurried along for a few hundred feet, then settled down to a more sedate pace about fifty feet behind the man under suspicion.

CHAPTER V.

NEW COMPLICATIONS.

THE Russian seemed to be in no hurry. He walked leisurely along, glancing up at the store signs, his face twisted in an ugly scowl. He paused just outside a gas station on the corner, seemed to deliberate for a moment, then strode over and accosted the attendant. Ted lounged forward, pretending to be interested in everything but this man he had been following. It took him a little while to jockey to a position close enough to hear what was being said. The man's voice came clearly to his ears:

"Thees gentleman is tall, thin, very striking in appearance. He has a close moustache which has turned to gray. Sometimes he wear gold-rimmed spectacles. His hair stand straight up like a broom. Have you seen such a man, monsieur? Once you see him, you would never forget. No doubt, he would come in a party with other men—Japanese, I think —in a large green car."

The Russian fixed the station attendant with a glassy, piercing stare and demanded fiercely:

"You tell me quick! Have you seen either thees man or the Japanese or the green car?"

"I didn't notice particular," replied the man at the oil station, shaking his head. "I don't never pay much attention to cars that pass here anyways. Mebbe if such a party had stopped, I'd have got 'em more clear in my mind."

Greatly disappointed, Ted slouched back toward the sidewalk, hands thrust deep in his pockets.

"Pshaw!" he muttered angrily. "That fellow's on the same errand that we are. He's looking for Professor Valdmere too. That description he gave to the attendant fitted the professor to a T. Gee whiz, I wonder what we'll discover next?"

However, the Russian had imparted a bit of information that Ted considered might be of value to them in the search. It was that Professor Valdmere would be in a green car and accompanied by a party of Japanese. What reason had the man to think so? What was the fabric of the plot that had woven its threads of mystery and intrigue through the pattern of the Professor's life? It was all very confusing and perplexing. Ted had now begun to realize that the trouble into which the famous scientist had been plunged was of no ordinary kind.

Still puzzling deeply, he retraced his way back along the street, his face very grave and solemn. He hated to rejoin Philo and Miss Valdmere and report that nothing had come of his efforts to shadow the suspicious-looking foreigner. He dreaded to think of the great disappointment that this admission would bring to the girl. Already nearly frantic with grief and worry, he feared that she might break down completely.

When he reached the car, to his astonishment, he found that it was unoccupied. Neither was their any trace of Philo and the girl. He glanced up along the street expectantly. They were in a store perhaps. No doubt they would return in a few minutes. They had agreed to meet him here. Then suddenly his eyes bobbed wide open, his heart quickening its beat.

Attached to one of the levers under the steering wheel, was a small piece of paper bearing a message of some sort. He snatched it up eagerly and read:

"Gone on a hot clue here in Langdon. Wait here until we return. Philo."

Ted gasped as he crumpled the paper in his hand.

"Great Cæsar, what next. Wish I'd got back in time to join them."

Scowling lightly, he climbed into the front seat and had barely taken up his position behind the wheel when he heard the voice of someone standing close beside the car. Involuntarily a sharp exclamation escaped him and he sat there staring straight into the sinister eyes of the man he had just been shadowing.

"What ess eet you do here, my young friend?"

"I'm no friend of yours," Ted glared back at him.

"Pardon. So monsieur has joined the chase too. One of the young men who sleep in my room at ze hotel. Where ees eet the other?"

The anger and resentment that the fellow's presence had inculcated began to sweep through Ted with such driving force that he felt like stepping out of the car and engaging his unwelcome visitor in a physical combat.

"I don't think it is any of your business where my friend is. And if you don't mind, you'll leave here at once and attend to your own affairs. I have no wish to talk to you."

At this the foreigner became slightly menacing. He strode closer, threw one arm over the side of the car and stood there, his countenance distorted in an ugly grimace.

"At least monsieur ees frank," he purred. "But when you say eet ees not my business, you guess wrong. Also if monsieur know what ees healthy for him, he will keep out of thees. Do I make myself understood?"

"Perfectly," faltered Ted. "I understand you," his hands clenched, "but you're wasting your breath. My advise to you is to trot along before I call the police."

The Russian stepped back and bowed profoundly.

"You have make your decision quickly, my friend. Eet ees cross swords then. You are not afraid?"

"Not in the least," lied Ted. "You can't frighten me." Then impertinently, "Good-bye."

The other bowed again and stepped back to the curb. Without once looking back, he walked a short distance along the street and entered a store. Not until then did the young man's muscles relax and his face resume an expression more becoming to it.

He slouched further down in the seat, mentally digesting this new phase to an already perplexing and seemingly unsolvable mystery. How long he sat there he did not know. For a long time the minutes dragged themselves along unnoticed. Presently, he aroused himself and looked at his watch. It was twenty minutes past nine, time that Philo and Miss Valdmere were returning. What was keeping them?

Beginning to be worried, he quit the car and commenced wandering nervously up and down the street in the hope of seeing them. A crowd of country folk gaped at him during his aimless journeying. Very slowly his patience had become exhausted. Fight as he would against it, he was annoyed with Philo for departing in this unceremonial manner, leaving behind him an unsatisfactory note that gave no hint as to their whereabouts.

"At least they might have told me where they were going," grumbled Ted, his eyes squinting in the glare of the sunlight that now poured down the uninviting thoroughfare. "Now what do you suppose he meant by a hot clue?"

Still puzzling, he went into a drug and confectionery store and ordered an ice cream. There were, perhaps, not more than four or five persons sitting in the little booths that ran along one side of the room. He chose a table in front, facing the door. In this way he had a good view of the street. He wanted to be sure not to miss Philo and Miss Valdmere.

He had finished his ice cream and had risen to pay the cashier at the counter, when his attention was attracted by a green car that purred along the hot asphalt and became lost to view.

He was not quite sure, but in the fleeting glimpse that he had had of the occupants of the car he could have sworn that they were Japanese!

CHAPTER VI.

AN UNEXPECTED MEETING.

JAPANESE! A green car! Ted rushed over, slammed his money down on the counter and darted out to the sidewalk in an effort to find out where the car had gone. It was just turning a corner down at the far end of the main street. Realizing that not a moment was to be lost, he ran back to Miss Valdmere's car, jumped in and hurried away in hot pursuit.

He overtook his quarry within three blocks. The Japanese delegation had pulled in to one side of the road and two of their members alighted and were now confering with the blue-coated figure of Langdon Prairie's only policeman. While still a block away, Ted had made his plan. He, too, drew to the same side of the street, shut off his motor and hopped out. Walking slowly, he approached the three men, the town constable and the two Japanese. Ears alert as he came within hearing distance, he could hear the Japanese spokesman, a dapper little fellow, speaking in a melodious voice, using perfect English.

"We have reason to believe that a tall, thin man, past midle age, white hair and a closely cut mustache, came to this town sometime early this morning in company with two Russians, rather repulsive-looking men. They were driving a large gray car, a sedan. Did you see anything of them?"

"Can't say that I did," Ted heard the constable answer. "Anyway—" a little belligerently, "what about it?"

"It is very important that we should find the man whose description we have given you."

"What's his name?" blurted out the constable.

The Japanese replied in so low a voice that Ted, who had already passed them, could not hear the answer. But a moment later, he did hear the Japanese thanking the officer of the law. Taking a hasty look back over his shoulder, he saw them jump into their car and depart. No sooner had the big green automobile disappeared around the next corner than he, too, was accosting the policeman.

"The two Japanese whom you were speaking with just now were making inquiries about the same person that I am trying to find."

So surprised was the guardian of law and order of Langdon Prairie that he choked and nearly swallowed a fresh cud of tobacco.

"You!" he exclaimed, his watery, blue eyes giving Ted a swift appraisal that ran from head to foot.

"Yes, sir. I am looking for the same man. A friend of mine and this man's daughter, Miss Valdmere, are in my party."

"Valdmere!" the constable's jaws suddenly clamped. "Yer mean that crazy professor chap what's been doin' all them queer things over at Brownvsille?"

"Yes, sir," said Ted again.

"But why are they looking fer him?"

"For the same reason that we are, I suppose. He has disappeared. There is every reason to believe that he was forcibly taken from his estate early this morning. His daughter was the first to discover that he had gone and set out here in search for him. She found a bit of paper in his office with the name of this town written upon it. She believes he was forcibly taken from his office by a desperate band of men. A safe was also blown open and part of its contents stolen."

"The motive was robbery then," gasped the astute and still gaping upholder of the law.

"I dare say," said Ted.

The constable whittled off another chew of tobacco from a convenient plug, staring at Ted thoughtfully.

"If I'm gonna help you, I'd like to get particulars

first hand from this young lady what you claim is
the professor's daughter. If you don't mind, you
can drive me over to where she is an' I'll have a
talk with her."

Ted explained that Miss Valdmere and Philo
had hurried away on an important errand but that
he expected them to return shortly. He handed him
the note which had been left in the car by his chum.
The other examined it with interest.

"Who's this man Philo?" he grunted, studying
the signature,

"He's my friend, the one I spoke of," replied Ted.
"Miss Valdmere is with him. They were waiting
for me to return from an errand. From what it
says, I understand they've picked up a clue."

"A hot clue," read the constable.

"Yes, according to Philo. But they're here in
Langdon Prairie somewhere and should be back
soon."

"How long have they been away?" came the next
question.

Ted looked at his watch. "A little over an hour
now."

The constable glared over his spectacles and spat
in the dust of the street. He delivered himself of an
ultimatum:

"Well, there ain't nothin' to be gained by sittin'
here. It's up to us to get busy. I reckon that you're

friends is so plumb occupied right now that they ain't even thinkin' about comin' back.   My suggestion is to drive 'round the town an' keep on drivin' till we find a trace of 'em."

The suggestion was immediately acted upon. They moved out into the increasing traffic of Langdon Prairie's main street and, with the constable pointing out the way, commenced driving about the town.   For twenty minutes they drove steadily. They were completing the third lap around the village's residential section, when, glancing up in the mirror in front of him, Ted saw the reflection of a gray car speeding along close behind them.   He recognized the driver at once.   It was the Russian.

Cheeks flushing with anger, Ted stared his defiance through the mirror and put on speed.   But to no avail.   The gray car continued to keep close behind him.   In desperation, finally, he drew in to the side of the street and came to a sudden, jarring stop.   The gray car stopped, too.   The policeman stared at Ted in amazement.

"What's the big idea?" he inquired.

"Look behind you."

The constable turned his head and scowled back. For a space of probably two minutes he forgot to chew his tobacco.   His hand whipped inside his blouse and came out holding a deadly-looking six-gun. Mumbling something to Ted, he clambered out of the car.

Whatever other qualifications the constable might have lacked, courage was not one of them. Heels striking heavily along the gravelled road, he proceeded straight back to the occupants of the second car and demanded an explanation.

"You're gonna stop followin' us or I'll know the reason why," he concluded.

"If the young man do not wish to incur trouble," calmly replied the driver of the gray car, "you can tell heem not to interfere in matters not his own. An' what I say about heem applies to you also."

Ted did not hear the constable's reply. It was drowned in a splitting roar similar to that made by an exploding tire. His first impression was that the policeman had fired point-blank at the insolent Russian. He felt suddenly so weak and dazed that he had scarcely the strength to turn his head. Then as if in a dream, he heard the grinding of gears, saw the gray car leap out into the road past the prostrate figure of the constable lying in the road, and then quickly ducked his head. A bullet zipped past him, smashing the windshield. A fragment of flying glass cut the back of his head.

The gray car disappeared in a furious cloud of dust. He could hear people running, saw the constable wriggling there in the road and, stumbling out of the car, he ran back and raised the wounded man's head.

"Where are you hit?" he choked.

The constable opened his eyes but did not reply. Others were around them now staring open mouthed. A big man assisted Ted to carry the policeman to Miss Valdmere's car, puffing as he did so.

"We must get Mr. Colby to the hospital. I'm afraid he's badly wounded. I'll go with you and show you the way."

CHAPTER VII.

PHILO'S HOT CLUE.

IT was just ten o'clock by Ted's watch when he left the Langdon Prairie Hospital after hearing the verdict of the physician who had examined the unconscious Colby. It was a different Ted than the one who had risen so cheerily that morning, unaware of what the day had in store. Altogether, it had been an exciting, thrilling four hours. Looking back over the events that had taken place during that time, it seemed incredible that so many mysterious happenings could have been crowded into so short a space. It had all tended to confuse and bewilder him. Almost staggering down the hospital steps toward the street, his thoughts were whirling dizzily. He scarcely heard the voice of the big man who had assisted him in bringing the constable to the hospital.

"He was pretty lucky at that," the voice ran on. "If that bullet had gone an inch further to the right, Colby would have been killed instantly. He has a chance, a fighting chance, the doctor said."

"I—I'm glad," stammered Ted. "I suppose I ought to be glad that they didn't kill me too. I must hurry and take you home and try to find my friends," he concluded.

"What is all this trouble about?"

"I really don't know myself," replied Ted as they got into the car. "We were trying to find two friends of mine when we saw this car following us. Constable Colby went back to order them not to do so when they deliberately fired upon him. That's about all I know."

"You mean that's all you care to tell me," said the big man, smiling queerly at Ted.

Ted flushed. "It would take too long to go into all the particulars. All I care to say now is that Professor Valdmere has disappeared and that my friend and myself are trying to find him."

"Professor Valdmere was giving some sort of a demonstration at Brownsville, wasn't he?"

"Yes, that was his intention. But it seems there's a conspiracy against him. We have reason to believe that he was brought here to Langdon Prairie."

The big man was pondering over this information when Ted stopped the car at the scene of the recent encounter with the Russians and his passenger got out. Just before turning to make his way up to his own house, he held out his hand to Ted.

"I don't understand it all, but I wish you all the

luck in the world. Here's hoping that you find Professor Valdmere."

"Thank you," returned Ted, struck with the sincerity in the other's voice. "We'll certainly do all we can to find the professor and bring his captors to justice. Good morning, sir."

"Good morning," smiled the man.

Ted drove on. In a few more minutes, he was back to the same place where they had originally parked their car. To his unutterable joy, he saw Miss Valdmere standing near the edge of the curb waiting for him. No sooner had he driven up beside her than she gave a little cry of welcome and hurried toward him.

"Oh, Mr. Winters," she declared, her lips trembling, "I thought you'd never come. We must hurry. There isn't a moment to lose. Your friend, Mr. Philo Birch, is in grave danger."

She had clambered into the seat beside him and one hand rested agitatedly upon his arm.

"I'll show you the way. Straight to the west side of town—a little house just on the outskirts. Oh please hurry, Mr. Winters!"

Trembling with eagerness, Ted backed the car away from the sidewalk, then put it into forward gear. Speeding down the street and taking the first turn to the right, they raced like mad.

"Hurry—hurry—hurry!" sang out the girl

almost hysterically. "I think that Father is in that house."

"But Philo——"

Three men came out to grab him when he crept up to investigate. I was standing back by the gate and just as soon as I saw that, I turned and ran for my life."

"What did these men look like?" asked Ted.

"There were three desperate looking men. I really can't describe them."

"But how did you happen to go there in the first place?" puzzled Ted. "What led Philo to believe that he had struck a hot clue?"

"It wasn't Philo. It was I. We were sitting there waiting for you, when a man, very nicely dressed, a Japanese, passed along the street right in front of us, carrying a portmanteau. It was in black leather with a silver clasp. Down in one corner, in small silver letters, were the initials C. C. V. It was the one I had given father last year for Christmas and I knew that I couldn't be mistaken. Father kept it in his office and, of course, the thieves took it. So I told Philo, I mean Mr. Birch, and we got out of the car and followed him. We kept about a block behind him and he led us straight to this little shack to which we're proceeding now. We watched the man go inside. Then, after a time, your friend, Mr. Birch, asked me to wait for him near the gate while he went forward to reconnoitre. He wanted to look through the window to see if Dad was there."

Ted's eyes were shining. "Miss Valdmere," he announced, "I believe that you have stumbled upon a real clue. That man who carried the portmanteau must know of your father's whereabouts. Was he one of the three who came out and overpowered Philo?"

She shook her head. Then, suddenly, her hand gripped his shoulder.

"Slow down!" she instructed excitedly. "There's the place!"

Not only did Ted follow out these orders, but he stopped altogether. Turning in the seat, he faced the girl.

"Now, Miss Valdmere, I'll tell you what I propose to do. It would be folly to go over there unarmed, so to make sure that I have a chance to rescue your father and Philo, I'm going to secure a weapon from some person in this neighborhood. It will be necessary for me to explain that your father and my chum are being held prisoners there. I shall tell them about my experiences with Colby. You don't know anything about that yet, but I'll tell you later. Will you wait here in the car or would you rather go along with me?"

"I think I'll go with you," replied Miss Valdmere.

At the first place a woman opened the door, regarding them with ill-concealed distrust. When Ted had explained his errand, she shook her head and slammed the door.

"I won't be no party to such goings-on," they heard her shrill voice on the other side of the barrier. "I don't believe a word of it anyway."

Ted looked at Miss Valdmere and Miss Valdmere looked at Ted. The young lady wrinkled her nose and sniffed.

"Come on, Mr. Winters," she said haughtily, "we'll go to the next place."

Here they found a more sympathetic audience. The man of the house, an honest-looking young fellow of perhaps thirty or thirty-five years of age, clad in a pair of unionalls and with a grease smudge on his right cheek, heard them through and immediately came to their rescue.

"Sure I got a gun. A shotgun an' a rifle. An' what's more, stranger, I'm gonna lend you a hand. Colby is a friend o' mine, an' I'm sure sorry to hear that he got hurt. Won't you stay here, Miss," he turned to the girl, "while me an' your friend go over an' find out what's what? It ain't no job for a woman."

Miss Valdmere hesitated, looked at Ted, puckering her pretty mouth.

"I'd like to go, too, if you'd let me," she beseeched them. "I'll promise to stay 'way behind and not get into any danger. I just know Father is there. I can't wait until you capture those men and release him."

So it was agreed. Miss Valdmere accompanied Ted and his new-found friend to the end of the block. Holding their weapons in readiness, the two advanced.

"Who lives in that house?" inquired Ted.

"Nobody. It's been empty for weeks. It's just a shack and it's difficult to find a renter."

They reached the gate without mishap. It stood partially open, swinging on rusty hinges. The two advanced within the yard.

"There's a window on the right side," explained the mechanic. "I'll sneak around to the front while you go to that window. Just as soon as I knock, smash in the glass with the end of your gun barrel and threaten to blow them into Kingdom Come."

Trembling and shaking in every limb, Ted made his way to the place designated and stood there waiting for the signal. Presently it came—a loud knock, repeated several times, then a voice calling out harshly:

"Open up or we'll fire!"

At that instant Ted leaped, jabbing fiercely at the glass which splintered around him. He called out in a shaking voice:

"Open the door. I have you covered."

The door did not open. No sound issued from within. An unusual silence had followed the smashing of the glass. A sudden realization came over Ted and he leaned forward dizzily, grasping the ledge of the window for support.

"Too late!"' he mumbled in a choking, agitated voice. "They're gone!"

CHAPTER VIII.

THE HILLS' ROAD.

DISCOURAGED and beaten, for a full minute Ted stood, gazing through the shattered window into the empty room. He had just stepped back to make his way around to the front, when the young mechanic came bounding to meet him.

"They've made their getaway," he shouted. "Not even a trace of them!"

Disheartened, they went back to the corner, where Miss Valdmere joined them. No need for her to ask what had happened. It was all revealed in Ted's face, his drooping shoulders, his haggard, dejected manner.

"They're gone!" cried the girl, choking back a sob. "Oh, Mr. Winters—Ted!—What shall we do now?"

Hayward, the young mechanic, who had accompanied Ted to the shack, came forward at this juncture with a suggestion that helped to brighten their outlook.

"Well, you mustn't lose heart, Miss," he consoled

her. "There's a pretty good chance that someone in this neighborhood saw them crooks when they left the shack and'll be able to tell us which direction they went." He turned to Ted. "If you'll take this young lady back to the car, I won't be more than a few minutes making inquiries."

Smiling cheerfully, Hayward left them. Turning with laggard steps, Ted and the girl made their way back to the car. Very little was said. Despite his effort to look on the bright side of things, he was horribly depressed. Every minute, so it seemed, they were plunging deeper and deeper into trouble and misfortune. Not only Professor Valdmere, but his own chum, Philo, was now in the toils of the gang. He cast a covert glance at the girl and noticed, with a tug at his heart, that her eyes were stained with tears. Arriving at the car, they clambered in, Ted putting his borrowed rifle in the back seat. They had waited only a short time when Hayward returned.

"Just like I thought," he informed them in a hearty voice. "Mrs. Holland, a widow, living in that little cottage over there,"—pointing—"seen 'em go. They ain't got more than a half hour's start on you either. They had a big touring car and went straight out on the Hills' Road. You got a pretty good chance to overtake 'em."

"Is there another town between here and the foot-hills?" inquired Ted breathlessly.

"Nary a one. The farther you go, the fewer houses you'll see. The hill country ain't fit for nothin' but sheepherdin' an' there's mighty little of that. Here an' there, mebbe, you'll run across a sheep camp or see a fire ranger. But fer the most part, that district ain't changed any since the days when the Indians was here. I'd go along with you, but I'm workin' at a garage down town, and' I'd have to ask permission to get away. Howsoever, I'm lendin you that rifle till you get back. Mebbe you'll need it," he finished grimly.

"Thank you very much," said Ted. "Both Miss Valdmere and myself appreciate your kindness. There's one question I'd like to ask you: Is the road a good one?"

"It's fair for a long ways," the mechanic answered. "But after that it ain't so good. Mostly up an' down. After a time it'll end altogether an' you won't see nothin' but pack trails, branching away through the scrub and amongst the rocks. I don't figure that party will try to climb the mountains beyond, so your chances is pretty good."

"I'm glad to hear you say so."

Just as Ted started the car, Miss Valdmere opened her purse, extracted a bill of large denomination and smilingly presented it to Hayward. In a

moment they were whirling away toward the Hills'
Road.

"Do you mind if I drive faster than we've ever
gone before?" Ted asked. "I want to try to make
up the time we've lost."

"Go as fast as you like," came the prompt answer.

The motor roared as they streaked across the
rolling prairie. The Hills' Road was narrow,
evidently an ancient highway, over which for several
generations the wagons of ranchers and home-
steaders had jarred and rumbled. Yet they contrived to make good time, mile after mile spinning
away behind them. It was apparent, however, that
the country was becoming rougher as they advanced.
Ted experienced a queer sensation as they fared
farther and farther from civilization into the bleak
and forbidding hills. There had been something
friendly and reassuring about the prairie, but these
rocks and gorges looked treacherous.

"Hope we don't have to go much farther west,"
he sighed to himself. "Don't like the lay of the
land here. Should have had an airplane."

"Mr. Winters?"

"Yes, Miss Valdmere."

"We've forgotten to bring food. It's just occurred to me. I haven't had a bite to eat all day."

Driving along, Ted considered this.

"We could stop at one of the ranches," he suggested.

"Perhaps later, but not now. I can stand it. Tonight, maybe, we'll come to a ranch where we can purchase a few supplies."

"I sincerely hope so," said Ted.

She lapsed into another long silence, watching the trail ahead. No longer did it go forward in a straight line. It curved and twisted and coiled its awkward way through the hills like a huge snake. Rounded buttes and shaggy rocks—there seemed to be no end to them. Ted was forced, finally to check his speed to a mere ten miles an hour. His wrists ached from holding the wheel.

He had coasted down a long hill and was part way up the second when the motor sputtered and died. Ted bit his lips in vexation. In their excitement and hurry they had forgotten not only food but gasoline as well. Out of gas and forty miles from nowhere!

Foot touching the brake to ease the backward roll of the car, they glided to the bottom, where, for a full minute, they sat thoughtfully staring at each other.

"Should have known better," Ted upbraided himself. "You'll think me an awful ninny, Miss Valdmere."

The girl set her mouth grimly. "It can't be helped

now. It's my fault as much as yours. The thing to consider is, what are we going to do?"

"Walk," said Ted laconically. "It's much slower but we'll get there. There's a chance, too, that many of these herders have cars and can sell us some gasoline."

"And if they haven't gasoline they'll probably have food," said Miss Valdmere brightening. "I'm not afraid to walk."

But if Miss Valdmere had known what lay behind the dark pages of the immediate future, she might not have faced the coming ordeal so calmly. They set out side by side, Ted with the rifle slung over his shoulder and the girl carrying her handbag. Descending a hill was not so difficult, but the ascent was wearisome. She wore high-heeled shoes. It was not long before her feet were torturing her. Time and time again, Ted was forced to assist her over rough ground. It soon became apparent to both of them that she could not continue much longer.

Topping a rise, they paused to rest for a moment in the cooling breeze. Between the buttes the sun was pitiless. Both were panting and eyed each other questioningly.

"No use, Miss Valdmere, you can't go on. We might as well face the facts. Would you be afraid to stay here while I went on to look for help?"

The girl did not reply. For a moment, she looked at Ted appealingly.

"If I take off my shoes and sit here and rest for a few minutes, I think I might be able to continue for another two or three miles. Then if we see no sign of a ranch or sheep camp, I'll be compelled to do as you say. I'm terribly afraid of all this loneliness but for Father's sake I think I could endure more."

"I like your spirit," approved Ted. "Let us hope that we find a camp. But you needn't worry about me deserting you. I wouldn't go very far away."

Following a fifteen minute rest, they went on again. Miss Valdmere was struggling more bravely now, though her efforts were torturing. Suddenly she released Ted's arm, shrank back against a ledge of rock, a low cry escaping her.

"Quick!" she pointed. "You're rifle!"

For a split second, Ted could perceive no danger. Flashing through his mind, there came the thought that perhaps Miss Valdmere had become unnecessarily alarmed, when unexpectedly he, too, saw the thing that had startled her. Twenty yards to his right, to one side of a clump of bushes, stood a tall, bearded, uncouthly-dressed denison of this unfriendly-looking land. Long hair hung over his shoulders and his eyes seemed to shine out at them through a mass of unkempt beard. Startled at first,

Ted gradually regained his composure and called out to him.

"Hello."

"Hello, thar," answered the man in a friendly voice.

"Can you tell us where we'll find the nearest ranch?"

The man laughed. "Thar ain't no ranches up here, I reckon. Just a few scattered sheep camps."

"Could you sell us some food?" next inquired Ted. "This young lady here hasn't eaten all day. We'v run out of gasoline. Our car's back along the road. Can you help us?"

The man slid down from his perch and advanced toward them. He strode awkwardly over, one hand tugging at his beard.

"Reckon I could help you if you're hard put," he told them. "I ain't got no gasoline, but I can stake you to a bite to eat. I got a bunch of sheep back here in the hills and a chuckwagon full of grub. You sure are welcome to it, stranger."

Ted's heart leaped with gratitude. Behind this man's rough exterior was a warm heart. He turned his head and smiled at Miss Valdmere.

CHAPTER IX.

CAMP OF THE SHEEPHERDER

ON the way over to the chuckwagon, the man explained that his name was Brent. He had been looking for some stray lambs, he said, and had come to the trail during his quest. He was glad now he had. Otherwise he might have missed them altogether.

"It's no fun," he told them gravely, "to get lost in these here hills."

"Probably we wouldn't get lost," Ted looked up at their benefactor. "We'd be all right as long as we stuck to the trail. We could always find our way back."

The sheepherder shook his head, smiling grimly.

"But that trail would have peetered out soon," he reminded him. "You see, it don't only go a few miles farther. The country in thar gets very rough and everything looks alike. Nobody ought to go up thar lest he had plenty of grub and was right handy findin' his way about. Seems like you two young uns was courtin' death to try and make it up thar on foot. Should have had a pack-horse anyways."

Miss Valdmere was very tired by the time they had reached the chuckwagon, but she brightened immediately at sight of food Brent brought out from the mysterious recesses of his covered wagon. Bacon, fresh mutton, beans, crisp, flaky crackers and tins of jam. Brent washed his hands at a little creek, near which he had made his camp, and set to work with a will. It was not long before dinner was ready.

Eating in the open with the faint aroma of wood smoke drifting around them, Ted thoroughly enjoyed the meal. Miss Valdmere ate heartily, too, praising Brent's efforts at cuisine.

"You're a wonderful cook," she told him. "I envy the rugged, healthy out-of-doors life you lead. I think I would be happy now if only you could tell us how we might continue with our journey."

The sheeperder looked up in surprise.

"You surely ain't plannin' to go on?" he gasped

"Yes," said Ted. "It's very important. Miss Valdmere is seeking her father, whom we have reason to believe was forcibly brought up here to the hills.

"You mean against his will?" Brent was scowling lightly.

"Yes, that is what we have reason to fear, Mr. Brent. My friend, Philo Birch, is also in the party.

Did you hear their car passing along the trail?"
Brent shook his head. "I can't rightly say. Most
of the morning I been 'way down the creek looking
for them lambs. 'Nother thing, my hearin' ain't so
good as it used to be. However, 'bout two hours
ago, I made out what looked like a cloud of dust."

"It must have been them," stated Miss Valdmere.

"And you're plannin' to follow them up?" came
the next query.

"That's what we had hoped, Mr. Brent. But
now," she sighed, her eyes downcast, "it begins to
look as if we will be compelled to give up the chase."

The sheepherder reached over and picked up the
coffee pot, simmering at the edge of the fire.

"Won't you have just one more cup?" he asked.
"This coffee'll plumb sure steady your nerves
Mebbe you're gonna need it. There ain't only one
way to get up into that thar country that bandit
car is ahittin' for, and that is with hosses."

"But where are the horses?" cried Miss Valdmere
and Ted in unison.

The sheepherder paused to brush away a crumb
that had fallen on the front of his shirt.

"There ain't any hosses," he replied, "except the
two I got picketted down there in the gully," he
pointed, "I use for drawing this wagon from place
to place."

"Oh!" said Ted, a little crestfallen.

"But you're welcome to them," continued the sheepherder.

Miss Valdmere smiled at their benefactor.

"It's very kind of you to make such an offer," she said. "But we really can't accept. You need the horses yourself. I couldn't think of depriving you of them. Thank you just the same."

The sheepherder brushed a few more crumbs from his faded blue shirt, glancing embarrassedly at the granite plate he held in his lap.

"That's perfectly all right, Miss. The only time I use them hosses, is when I saddle up and run into town or move this grub-wagon. When the grazing's good, like it is here, sometimes I don't move the wagon for several days. I just come over here this mornin' and the grass is good till Friday. I got plenty of grub, too, so you can use them hosses and are perfectly welcome to 'em till along about the end of the week."

Ted was about to decline the offer again when, upon second thought, he decided that it would be foolish. He and Miss Valdmere certainly needed the horses. If, by taking them they would not work a hardship upon the sheepherder, the logical thing would be to accept. They had already lost a good deal of time—and time was important. Nevertheless, he looked across at Miss Valdmere, a question in his eyes. To his relief, she addressed herself to

their uncouth but kindly-hearted host. Her face
lighted with another smile.

"Very well, Mr. Brent, I guess we'll have to take
them after all. But only on one condition."

"What's that, Miss?" asked Brent.

"That you'll permit us to pay for them."

"Not a cent," said Brent stubbornly. "You're
welcome to them."

"In that case we can't take them. It wouldn't be
fair to you. Something might happen to them and
us. That's the reason I'm offering to buy them."

Now it was evident from the expression on
Brent's face that the good man had supposed that
Miss Valdmere had offered to rent the horses, not
to buy them.

"Great Scott!" he said.

"We would want to buy them," insisted the girl.

Ted was surprised, too, until suddenly he remembered that this girl was the daughter of a
famous scientist—a man reputed to be very wealthy.
Naturally she would have plenty money of her own,
and would be only too willing to spend it in so
worthy a cause.

"We could sell them back to you upon our
return," she went on. "If we didn't get back, you
wouldn't be out very much. I'll pay you well for
them. Also, if you have them, a couple of saddles."

"I got two saddles," mused Brent. "If you want

to buy the hosses, Miss, that's a different matter. And you don't need to bother about returnin' them. I been figgerin' on selling this here team anyway. There's Strebbing, a friend of mine, coming over here tomorrow afternoon. He's the owner of the Circle W Ranch and has plenty of hossess and saddles, too." The sheepherder paused. "Now, Miss," he resumed, "if you was really plannin' on buyin' my two ponies, I'd take that money and have Strebbing fetch me over a couple more together with the saddles. Make me an offer on them."

"I haven't the faintest idea what they're worth. Name your own price."

"Two hundred and fifty dollars, including the saddles," said Brent promptly.

"I'll pay that," smiled Miss Valdmere. "But you'll have to accept my check. The bank in town will cash it for you."

"That's all right, Miss."

Miss Valdmere opened her purse, extracted a small check-book and a fountain pen and, soon afterward, presented a slip of paper to the somewhat bewildered Mr. Brent, who took it dazedly, folded it once across and hastily thrust it in his pocket. Then he rose, walked over to the wagon and procured two halter-shanks which he threw over his arm.

"I'll go down and get them ponies," he said,

"and bring 'em back and saddle 'em up for you."

He was away only for a few minutes, returning with two very presentable cow-ponies, one a sprightly little bay and the other a pinto, breathing fire, snorting as he came up.

"This one I call Star," indicating the bay, "and this pinto is Spitfire. If you ain't used to riding much, Miss, you'd better take the bay. He's gentle as a kitten. The pinto is gentle enough, too, but once in a while he gets ornery and is as full of tricks as a pesky coyote. Here, young man, you can hold the pinto while I saddle the bay. Too bad you ain't got ridin' skirts, Miss."

"It is too bad," agreed Miss Valdmere, "but it can't be helped. I'll ride side-saddle."

Ted had scarcely heard the conversation between Brent and Miss Valdmere, so interested was he in his own particular problem. He had never ridden a horse before in his life. He had always lived in the city and, though he had frequently seen others atop high-spirited mounts, he had never been permitted that experience himself. But now the opportunity had suddenly presented itself. No docile mount this, but a tricky, high-spirited broncho! He'd be compelled to watch him every minute. Once mounted, would he be able to retain his seat? Would the pony proceed to buck him off? He hoped not. It would make him look foolish in Miss Valdmere's eyes, whom he suspected was an expert rider. In silence he watched Brent saddle the two ponies. Absent-mindedly he shook hands with their bene-factor, watched Miss Valdmere leap lightly into the saddle, then gritting his teeth like one about to make a fateful plunge into a stream of ice-cold water, he thrust one foot into a stirrup and clambered clumsily up.

"Always take the reins before you mount," cau-tioned Brent.

"I'll try to remember," answered Ted between set lips.

An exchange of good-byes and they cantered away. Ted was thrilled. Although he bobbed about like a cork in water, he decided that this wasn't half bad. Some of his timidity left him. Suddenly he heard a shout. He looked back, saw that Brent was racing along on foot after them. He was about to draw rein, when Miss Valdmere called out to him sharply.

"Don't stop! Don't stop!" she cried.

"But—but why?" stammered Ted. "Mr. Brent must have forgotten something. He's calling to us."

He heard the girl's ringing laugh.

"That's all right. I know what he wants."

"What does he want?" asked the bobbing, young rider.

"He just found out," smiled Miss Valdmere, "that that check I gave him is made out for three hundred dollars instead two hundred fifty. We must pretend that we don't hear him. Don't look back."

Two hundred yards farther on, they slowed down to a walk as their course led down through a deep gully and thence on to the low-lying hills beyond.

"We're in luck," said Miss Valdmere.

CHAPTER X.

THROUGH THE HILL COUNTRY.

TED was chafed and sore before they had gone ten miles. He soon perceived that riding was not as easy as it looked. However, he had lost his fear of the pinto and had begun to suspect that Brent had exaggerated the pony's faults. Either that or Spitfire was on his good behavior. He neither shied nor balked.

"I think he'll be all right," said Miss Valdmere, "if you'll remember to keep a tight rein on him. Don't let him get his head down."

Ted had heard of bucking horses, but he had never seen one in action. He wondered about Spitfire. He laughed as he turned toward his companion.

"We're getting along nicely so far," he pointed out. "I don't really think that he is as bad as Mr. Brent has painted him."

"I wouldn't trust him too far," warned the other. "I know horses pretty well and I've invariably found that you can't trust an animal with eyes like that."

"They are tricky," admitted Ted. "But sometimes appearances are deceiving. I think Spitfire has taken a fancy to me."

The subject was promptly forgotten and they chatted of other things. The miles wore on. Ted became more and more weary and saddle-chafed. The sun beat down upon their heads with torrid heat, scarcely to be endured. The little valleys and gulleys which they repeatedly crossed or along which they made their way, all the while following the slowly dimming trail, were breathless, dazzling furnaces through which not even a faint breeze stirred. Being a much better horseman than Ted, Miss Valdmere pushed to the lead, setting a pace which Ted found difficult to follow. Long before the afternoon drew to a close, he was in misery, so stiff and sore that on several occasions it was only his pride that kept him from calling a halt.

As yet they had found no trace of Professor Valdmere's and Philo's captors. However, both felt that it wouldn't be long before they would. As Brent had expressed it, the trail was peetering out. It was barely a dim path now, threading its way through a region almost impossible for a car and it was getting rougher all the time.

"They'll be compelled to stop pretty soon," said Ted, looking away toward the gradually rising hills. No car in the world can climb those steep slopes. The very least they can do is to abandon it and proceed on foot. When they do that, we'll have the advantage and will be able to gain upon them rapidly."

"Unless," Miss Valdmere's voice sounded mournful, "they've laid their plans carefully in advance and have horses waiting for them."

"Let's hope they haven't," he replied.

And at that instant came the rabbit. Right at their feet he suddenly popped out of the brush and went bounding away to disappear along the rim of a gorge beyond. Ted could not explain afterward how it had all happened, but his next impression was of sailing through the air, scraping the top of a clump of brush and alighting with a crushing impact upon the rock-strewn ground beyond. The fall had dazed him and he lay, for a moment, quite unable to rise. In a sort of dream he saw the fiery-eyed pinto racing along the back trail, Miss Valdmere in hot pursuit. By the time he had clambered dizzily to his feet, they were nowhere in sight. A coulee had swallowed them up.

He stumbled forward a few paces, gasping for breath. He had lost the pinto! He really did not believe that Miss Valdmere would succeed in recapturing it. With only one pony now, how could they hope to overtake the bandits? Right at that moment things looked very bleak and discouraging for Ted.

For ten minutes he plodded along on the back trail, angry, saddle-chafed, despondent, upbraiding himself at every step. Into his mind had leaped another vision. Riding side-saddle and pursuing the bolting pinto over those treacherous rocks, it seemed very unlikely that Miss Valdmere, however dauntless and quick-witted she might be, could manage to retain her seat. He was sure that he would find her crushed and hurt somewhere back along the trail. The thought was appalling. It caused him to break into a run, tearing along in the direction the runaway had disappeared.

Unexpectedly his mouth snapped open. He could scarcely believe his own eyes. Nearly a quarter of a mile away, near a turn in the trail, he beheld Miss Valdmere returning, triumphantly leading the now penitent pinto. A wave of admiration for the girl's horsemanship and daring swept over him. He felt like a fool. It was a little hard to compare the frail young lady, who had fainted in the car, with this daring, brilliant equestrienne. When she approached closer, for the life of him, he could not raise his eyes to meet her sparkling glance.

"Are you very much hurt, Ted?" she asked.

"No. Shaken up, that is all. I feel like a fool, Miss Valdmere."

"Please don't call me Miss Valdmere any more," she upbraided him. "It sounds so—so upstage. Call me Margaret. Or better still, Peggy."

"Very well, Miss Val—I mean Peggy. And while I—I'm at it," he stammered, "I'd like to congratulate you. You're wonderful. I wish I could ride even half as well as you do."

"You'll learn, Ted. You can't expect to become proficient in just a few hours. But I'll say this for you, you've done remarkably well for a beginner. Now, if you don't mind, I'll dismount and take the pinto and you can take the bay."

Ted's face fell. "No," he said stubbornly, "I'll ride him myself."

"But it might happen again. It's almost sure to happen again. Spitfire has been startled and for the rest of the day he'll be hard to handle."

"I don't care," stormed Ted. "He can throw me a hundred times, but I'm going to stick to him. I intend to learn how to ride if it's the last thing I do."

"I admire your spirit," returned the girl, "but next time I might not be as fortunate in overtaking him. Goodness, how you limp. You're really hurt after all. Now don't try to deny it."

"It wasn't from being thrown," Ted answered quite truthfully. "I'm not used to riding and the motion has stiffened me up."

"We better rest here a while," suggested Miss Valdmere. "We——" her voice trailed off into a startled squeak.

Above the edge of a gully alongside the trail, a sinister head uprose. An ugly automatic pointed straight toward them.

"Stick 'em up!" snarled the voice.

One look at the menacing head and Ted's hand clawed the air. His cheeks blanched and, for the first time that day, he was stricken with a nameless terror. The man confronting him was the Russian who had previously threatened him and had later shot down Constable Colby at Langdon Prairie!

CHAPTER XI.

HOURS OF ANGUISH.

THE Russian's first act was to leap forward and remove Ted's rifle, strapped to the pinto's saddle. Then, holding both rifle and revolver, he turned upon his two shivering captives.

"Monsieur would not take hees warning," he leered. "Very well, we shall see what will come of eet. You have chose your own course. Now you may stand the consequences." To Miss Valdmere, "Dismount from your horse, mademoiselle."

White-faced, she hurriedly complied. Their captor half turned and waved his arm, calling out loudly in Russian. Immediately there came a hurried movement in the gully below and two other Russians, equally sinister, appeared over the edge of the yawning depression. The leader barked out orders to them in his gutteral, foreign voice.

Ted sensed what was coming. He and Miss Valdmere were tied hand and foot with the two halter shanks. Then the trio held a short consultation, occasionally turning to glower at their helpless captives. Finally the leader moved away from the others, advancing toward them. He bowed mockingly.

"Eet ees very good of monsieur and mademoiselle to help us out like thees. I thank you for the horses. Eet ees my wish that you rest quietly here while we go on. I am very sorry that I can spare no water or food for you."

"You mean that you are going to leave us here without food or water?" flamed Ted.

"You have guess correct."

"You brute!"

The Russian scowled. "You remember I warned you, monsieur. Thees ees no child's play. You elect to take the chance. Now you cry like a baby because fortunes of war did not go your way."

"I'm not crying," choked Ted. "And don't you ever think for one moment that I'm afraid of you. I'd die and rot here before you'd ever hear a murmur out of me. But any man who would bind up a young girl and leave here here under this glaring, hot sun with neither food nor water in an out of the way spot like this, is a despicable unnamed beast."

The Russian's leering half-smile vanished and in its place there leaped a dangerous look.

"Ted, Ted!" remonstrated Miss Valdmere.

The leader made a threatening move toward Ted,

changed his mind and stepped back, laughing coarsely.

"Eet ees mademoiselle's fault, not mine. If she chose to do a man's work she must expect a man's treatment. Again I wish to thank you for the horses."

With a mocking sweep of his hand, the Russian strode over, mounted the pinto, ordered one of his comrades to take the bay and the two set out. In that instant, Ted's heart leaped with hope. Perhaps the third man would be left to guard them. At any rate, he seemed to be in no hurry to go away. He sat down upon a rock, thrust a cigarette between his lips and puffed upon it idly. Occasionally, he looked across at the two prisoners, smiling to himself.

"Do you stay here?" asked Ted finally.

The Russian shook his head.

"You have food in your knapsack," said Ted. "Will you not leave us some?"

Again the man shook his head.

"I have a purse here," trembled Miss Valdmere, "with money in it. Leave food for us here and take my purse with you."

The Russian scoffed at the suggestion. He rose, walked to the edge of the gorge, threw his cigarette over the edge with a contemptuous snort of disdain, then turned and strode away in the direction his companions had taken. In the terrible silence that followed, his footsteps resounded loudly for a time, then were heard no more. Ted turned his head and glanced at Miss Valdmere.

"Well?" he said.

The girl strove to recover her composure. She bit her trembling lips and blinked her eyes to check the hot, scalding tears streaming down her face.

"It's horrible," she moaned. "We'll die here!"

"Please don't feel so badly, Miss Peggy. Everything looks black now but there must be a chance. In fact, I'm pretty sure that we'll get out of this."

"How?" she inquired.

"I'm going to untie your wrists with my teeth. It may take hours to do it, but I'm sure it can be done. In stories I've read of men who have escaped by untieing a rope with their teeth."

"This isn't a story," replied Miss Valdmere. "This is real life. Did you ever try to untie a rope with your teeth?"

"No," said Ted truthfully. "I never did."

"It will do no harm to try," Miss Valdmere sobbed a little, still blinking her eyes. "Poor Dad! I'm beginning to believe now we'll never reach him in time."

Ted sat up and looked about him. Twenty yards away, he noticed an upstanding projection of rock, near the base of which lurked a wedge-shaped area of cooling shade—a tiny oasis in the blinding glare around them. To his despairing companion he pointed it out.

"Look, Miss Valdmere—I mean Peggy—there's a bit of shadow if we can get to it. And I think we can. We'll roll over and over and over. We may hurt our arms doing so, but even that is better than this terrible heat. Once there, we can experiment with the rope."

It was really not as difficult as Ted had surmised. In a few moments, both had reached their objective. Ted's new friend brightened visibly.

"This is better," she cried. "Now I'll lay on my face while you try to untie the rope."

Long before Ted had made even a faint impression upon the knot, he was ready to swear eternal vengeance upon all authors whose heroes liberated themselves in this fashion. He decided that if he ever got out of this predicament alive, one of his first acts would be to write letters to the magazines, objecting to such a practice. He had succeeded only in making the knot a fluffy ball of fiber—a thing to conjure with. It was a double knot and was tied securely. His teeth were bleeding and his lips were swollen from continuous contact upon the rough strands of the rope. To make matters still worse, Miss Valdmere was tired of lying in such an awkward position and her wrists had begun to swell from the constant tugging at the rope.

"I've been at it over an hour," Ted cried with exasperation, "and it's worse now than when I started."

Miss Valdmere turned over on her side and looked at Ted, the beginning of a new horror in her eyes.

"I'm afraid there is nothing for us to do but to lay here and wait," she faltered. "Let's take turns shouting for help."

This they did. They shouted until their throats burned and they had become so hoarse that they could shout no more. The echoes, flying from rock to rock, mocked them. The moment they ceased, the terrible silence dropped down around them again, seeming like a ghostly presence. Yet they had been heard. Along the gully there came to them a faint scratching among the rocks. Then, presently, a coyote thrust up its head and came forward to within fifty yards of where they were, sat upon its haunches, regarding them curiously. Miss Valdmere gave a little scream of dismay.

"Oh, Ted," she gasped, "a wolf!"

"No," answered Ted. "It's a coyote. They are very cowardly—easily frightened. They'll not touch us as long as we're alive."

"Ugh!" said Miss Valdmere.

At the end of fifteen minutes, having satisfied his curiosity, the coyote turned and trotted away. But in a short time he was back again, a friend with him.

They were a disreputable-looking pair, scrawny and thin, red tongues dripping.

"If this keeps on," said the girl, "there'll be a pack here before night and then I'm not so sure they won't attack us."

Ted said nothing. He knew very little more about coyotes than he did about range horses. He glanced at the knot. Suddenly an idea came to him.

"I think I have it now!" he shouted. "Sit up, Miss Peggy, with your back toward mine and see if you can't untie the knot on my wrists with your fingers. I can't untie your knot now because it is so frayed and woolly."

This scheme might have worked had it not been for one thing. Miss Valdmere's wrists were swollen and her fingers were numb. It was a hard knot to untie. She was forced finally to admit defeat and, as she did so, again tears trickled from her eyes.

Ted was desperate. "There, there, Miss Peggy!" he attempted to cheer her. "Please don't cry! We mustn't give up hope yet. I have still another plan in view. I'm certain it will work, too. A few strands at a time I'll nibble through the rope that binds your wrists, much as a mouse or rat would do. Do you think you could stand the pain?"

Miss Valdmere hesitated. "My wrists ache dreadfully," she murmured, "but—but we'll have to do something, won't we?"

"I'm afraid, Miss Peggy, it's our only chance."

"For Father's sake, I could endure anything."

And endure it she did. Ted set to work. The task seemed endless. Strand by strand, a few coarse fibers at a time, he chewed his way through the rope. His gums and lips were bleeding freely by the time he had finished. But there was exultation in his heart—the recompense of achievement that more than made up for the agony he had endured—the great suffering that had been hers.

It was late now, darkness was enfolding the land, stars peeping down from the magic carpet of heavens, while from every direction rang out the unearthly, blood-curdling shrieks of coyote voices. Miss Valdmere raised her swollen hands above her head, glorying in this new freedom.

"Just as soon as circulation is restored and the numbness goes out of my fingers, I'll untie the other knots," she cried. "Then—then——"

Ted's quick ears had caught a suspicious sound coming from far below them in the gully. He leaned forward quickly, brushing against her shoulder.

"Hush! Hush!" he whispered. "I think I hear someone coming."

CHAPTER XII.

TED PLAYS A LONE HAND.

"PROBABLY a coyote," said Miss Valdmere.

"No," said Ted. "Whatever it is, it's making too much noise for a coyote. It might possibly be one of the Russians returning."

Miss Valdmere became visibly excited. "Oh!" she cried. "We must get away from here at once. Here, let me try to untie the rope binding your arms."

Leaning forward, she began working feverishly at the knot and had succeeded in untieing it by the time whoever was in the gully had commenced to clamber up the steep ascent. With his arms freed, Ted worked quickly, too, a growing fear upon him. When their legs were free, they groped to their feet, making their way along the edge of the gully.

"I'm sure it's one of the Russians," panted Ted. "The minute he gets up here, I think our best plan will be to descend into the gully ourselves, then climb up the opposite side."

"Haloo! Haloo!" shouted a voice.

It had a familiar ring to it.   Miss Valdmere
clutched at Ted's arm.

"Brent!" she gasped.

And the sheepherder it proved to be.   Turning
back, they met him just at the top of the gorge.   He
was astride a pony from which he dismounted and
in the darkness they could see him mopping his
perspiring brow.

"Good Gracious!   But I sure am glad I found
you.   Seems like I've been hours wandering about
through the darkness, hollerin' for you.   I suspected
you was in trouble, mebbe one of you hurt, and I
came out right away."

"What made you guess we were in trouble?"
asked Miss Valdmere.

"Why, naturally, I couldn't think anything else,"
explained Brent, surprise in his voice, "when this
here pony came back.   I figgered that this here
pinto had throwed the young man off and mebbe
he was hurt.   It was about seven o'clock when he
came tearing into camp like a young cyclone and
plumb scared to death.   It's a good thing he didn't
lose the saddle and none of the grub."

"Good Heavens!" gasped Ted.   "To think that
things turned out like that.   I was angry with the
pony once, but not any more.   Hope he killed that
Russian."

"Russian!" chortled the sheepherder.   "Young

feller, just what do you mean? I ain't heard nothin about no Russian."

Thereupon Ted related their experiences of the afternoon.

"Now," he concluded, "if there's anything to eat in that saddle-pack, Miss Valdmere and I will certainly be glad to see it. We're almost famished, and our throats are burning with thirst."

Mr. Brent was a man of action. In a moment he had untied the saddle-packs, throwing them at their feet and, with a brisk, "There's water back there about a quarter of a mile," he turned the pinto's head and was away in a flash. Miss Valdmere turned upon Ted.

"If there ever was an angel in disguise, he's one. He looks rough and uncouth, but he's a true gentleman at heart. Somehow he reminds me of the rugged country itself. Come on, Ted, let's eat."

And they were still eating when Brent returned. Dismounting quickly, he advanced, carrying a water bottle filled to the top. It was ice-cold and tasted like nectar from the gods. Miss Valdmere and Ted drained it to the last drop and yet their thirst was not quenched.

"Mr. Brent," said Miss Valdmere, "I don't know how we can ever thank you. I can't begin to tell you how happy I feel."

"You don't need to thank me," said the sheep- .

herder a little crossly. "I've been well paid for this. I ain't forgot about that check. You made it out for three hundred dollars and I said only two hundred and fifty. I'm going to give you back every cent of that fifty. I've got it here in my pocket and —and——"

"Mr. Brent," she interrupted, "if it were a thousand instead of fifty dollars, it wouldn't repay you for the great service you have rendered us."

"Indeed not," agreed Ted.

"And we're not going to quarrel now," she hurried on, patting the sheepherder's arm. "You must keep that money and feel that you have earned it all."

"I won't never forget this, Miss," stated Brent. "I guess the thing to consider now, is what you two young uns are going to do."

"We must push on," Ted told him.

"With only one pony?"

"Miss Valdmere can ride and I will walk."

In the starlight, the sheepherder stroked his beard, gazing out over the scarred and broken region known as the hill country. When he spoke again, his voice was grim.

"You'll pardon me saying so, Miss, but this ain't the sort of work for a frail, young lady like you. You can never stand it. It ain't only the danger you're runnin' from them bandits, but there's terrible hardships in store for you every foot of the way. If you'll take my advice, you'll reconsider like and let this young man go alone. There's only one horse anyway. Let him ride it. That way he can make much better time than if you was to go along. The way I got it all figgered out, hurry means everything to you. I'll help you back to my camp and you'll be safe there."

"I can't! I can't!" protested the girl. "I must go on! I must find Dad! I—I——"

"Peggy," cut in Ted, "I think Mr. Brent is right. It's for your father's sake. It will only delay matters if the two of us go."

"And that ain't all, Miss," the sheepherder hurried on. "If you'll only go back with me and sort of look after things, I'll rush over to Strebbing's ranch and organize a sort of posse among the boys there to go to this young fellow's aid."

"I'll do it," trembled Miss Valdmere, "but—oh, if you only knew how hard it was. I won't rest. I won't sleep until—until I know that Dad is safe."

"We know how you feel," said Ted, placing a comforting hand upon her trembling shoulder.

"Yes, Miss, we'll start back at once and let this young man hurry after them bandits." Then to Ted, "You'll take good care of yourself, won't you? Watch the pinto and keep a tight rein. Don't run into no unnecessary danger till the right time comes.

Tomorrow sometime, me and a posse will be with you.''

A suspicious moisture in his eyes, a lump in his throat, Ted gripped the hand of the sheepherder and then bade farewell to Miss Valdmere. Then, unable to say another word, he clambered into the saddle, turned the pinto's head toward the west and rode out through the obscuring shadows that blanketed the earth. Once he turned his head and looked back. Darkness all around him, the distant, mournful cry of a coyote, an inutterable loneliness tugging at his heart.

When day broke, he was still in the saddle, traversing as forlorn and weird a country as his eyes had ever looked upon. All around him towered the hills, awful in their loneliness and silent grandeur. Nowhere could he see a sign of human habitation nor of humans themselves. If the bandits had come this way, they had left no trail. Picking his course down through a lonely looking valley, he picketted out his pony and sat down to a lonely breakfast. He ate with his eyes ever on the alert. And it was well that he did, for, just as he rose to go over to the pinto, far up on the distant slope of the valley, he saw the figure of a man.

CHAPTER XIII.

A GAME OF HIDE-AND-SEEK.

TED's first thought was that he had approached close to the camp of the bandits. He had no desire to meet any of them. He was unarmed and in no position to carry on open warfare. It was out of the question to hope that he could overcome any of the guards holding Professor Valdmere and Philo. If he succeeded in effecting their release, it would have to be by stealth. He must try to keep hid. At that distance away, the man descending into the valley might consider that he, Ted, was some wandering cowboy out in the hills searching for strays. To remain here and meet the man might prove fatal to his plans.

He mounted Spitfire and had started to ride leisurely away in the opposite direction when, casting a furtive look back, he saw the man waving his hands and running toward him. Acting upon the impulse of the moment, he drew in his horse and paused. Through his mind there ran a train of conflicting emotions.

Should he go on?

Finally caution won. Putting heels to his horse, he dashed up along the valley slope, cut through a narrow plateau, scattered with bolders and partially overgrown with sickly-looking scrub pine, then descended into a hollow depression on the farther side where the brush grew in wild profusion.

A plan had slowly formulated. He trembled with eagerness. Dismounting, he tied Spitfire securely in one of the thickest clumps and began retracing his steps cautiously on foot. Wherever it was possible, he darted from cover to cover, making his way back toward the valley. His intention was to spy upon the lone traveller. If it could be done expeditiously, he'd creep up through the rocks to get a good look at the man. He'd soon determine whether or not he was a bandit. If he was, the chances were that the fellow would be armed. Ted hoped so, because he had fully determined to creep up, spring out suddenly and try to disarm him. With a weapon in his possession, the release of Professor Valdmere and Philo would be much more simple.

By the time he had reached the valley's edge, far below he could see the moving figure of the man. He was in the open now, proceding straight across the valley toward Ted. Down, about thirty feet from the floor of the valley were a number of gigantic boulders that offered an excellent place for concealment. He had plenty of time to slip down there before the other could arrive. Then, if the man did not deviate from his course, he must of a necessity pass within a few yards of the spot Ted had picked out for his hiding place.

Tremendously excited now, he worked his way down the slope, never rising to his full heighth, descending from cover to cover. Without mishap, he reached his destination, slipped in behind a rock which, by raising to his tip-toes, he could see over, and slunk down, steeling himself for the coming ordeal.

The man was still quite a distance away, and several minutes must elapse before he could arrive. Ted mopped his brow and waited. He was so nervous that his hands shook. Never before had he been placed in such trying circumstances. Never before had he known what it was to lie in wait for one of his fellows. Whatever happened, he must try to keep a cool head. A great deal depended upon the outcome of that meeting. If the person, advancing across the valley straight toward him, proved to be one of the bandits—and there was every reason to believe that he was—he must contrive somehow not to fumble the job.

The moments that passed seemed without end. He crouched there, ears alert. With burning eyes, he looked at his watch. He clamped his jaws tightly while every nerve in his body seemed to tingle from the inactivity and suspense.

Across the silence broke the sound of moving feet. Ted darted up, gave one quick glance over his rocky barrier and perceived with a wildly beating heart that the bandit would pass straight up along a narrow defile within a very few feet of him. It was patent that the thing to do was to slip over behind another rock near which the man must pass.

Nerves atingle, he slipped over to the edge of the defile and waited. The noise made by his adversary grew louder. He could hear the man's feet scraping over the rocks. He could hear the man's breath. Presently, a few inches of the man himself came within his line of vision and he leaped, as a tiger might have leaped from its hiding place in the jungle. The feet of Ted's opponent flew out from under him and the forms of both went crashing back amongst the rocks. Following the first shock, Ted half scrambled up, feeling for the weapon. But in that moment, his eyes caught sight of his antagonist's face and his arms seemed to freeze at his sides and his stomach to roll over sickeningly. Involuntarily, he uttered a cry that might have been heard half across the valley.

"Philo!"

But Philo had been dazed by the fall and he lay back, eyes closed, shaken and helpless. For one

awful moment, Ted actually believed that he had
crushed out the life of his own chum. A new horror
flooded his mind. He began to whimper and gibber
like one bereft of his senses.

Then Philo opened his eyes and a wave of color
flowed back into his pallid cheeks. He mumbled,
threw out his arms, groped to a sitting position,
whereupon Ted darted forward, steadying him with
a supporting arm.

"Oh, Philo, I'm so sorry," he wailed. "Thought
you were one of the bandits. I'm so happy, Philo.
How did you manage to escape? Where is the
professor? Did they mistreat you, Philo?
How——"

"Good gracious," interrupted Philo, "one question
at a time—please! Say, you are a chump. And
now that we're in this business of asking questions,
I guess I have a right to a few myself. How in
the dickens did you get here? Where is Miss Valdmere? Thought you were back in Langdon Prairie."

"We discovered you had come this way and followed you," answered Ted. "Miss Valdmere is safe.
Right now she is staying at a sheepherder's camp
about thirty miles east of here. I hurried on in the
hope that I might find your party and in some way
effect your release."

"We succeeded in making our escape last night,"
explained Philo in a matter-of-fact tone as if he were

refering to a most trivial commonplace. "Last night
we got away," he repeated, "and believe me, we
earned our freedom. We knocked down two of the
guards and, I think, Professor Valdmere must have
killed a third. We were pursued through the dark
and, on three different occasions, we were almost
recaptured."

"But where is Professor Valdmere now?" Ted
interrupted.

"I don't know."

"You don't know!" gasped Ted.

"No, I don't——" a little testily. "We became
separated in the dark. He's around in these hills
somewhere. All this morning I've been searching
for him but I haven't seen a soul, not one, except
a man on horseback who wouldn't stop when I
waved to him."

Ted grinned a little sheepishly. "I was that man,"
he said.

"But why didn't you stop?"

"Because I suspected you might be one of the
bandits. I wasn't armed and was taking no chances.
I hid my pony in some brush and then came back
here hoping that I might overpower the man and
secure his weapon."

Philo scowled. "Well, you certainly overpowered
me. But anyway, Ted, I'm glad that I found you
and that you can give me a hand in locating Pro-

fessor Valdmere. By the way, have you anything
to eat? I'm hungrier than a bear. I haven't had
a bite since we escaped. One can't live on nothing
but water."

Ted helped Philo to his feet.

"You bet, I've something to eat. Come with me.
It's back in the saddle-pack. While we're on the
way there, I want you to tell me about this gang
that captured Professor Valdmere. Who are they?
What is their motive? How many are in their
party? It's all a big mystery to me and I won't rest
until I get all the details."

"Well you won't get any of the details until I
have appeased the inner man. It's a long story and
I'm too hungry and tired now to tell it to you. How
far is your pony from here?"

"Not over a quarter of a mile," replied Ted, helping his chum up the steep incline to the top of the
valley wall.

In silence, they crossed the plateau and made their
way down the brush-covered depression. Spitfire
raised his head above an obstructing brush and
snorted.

"Cracky!" Philo cried out. "Where did you get
hold of that wild-looking outlaw?"

"Miss Valdmere purchased him from a sheep
rancher named Mr. Brent at the place where she is
now stopping. She bought another pony, too, but

that one is now in the hands of that Russian who slept in our room at the Grand Majestic Hotel."

While he was speaking, Ted walked in through the brush, removed the two saddle-packs which he threw over his shoulder and bore to his hungry companion.

"Now, Philo," he cried out jokingly, "you can hop to it and eat to your heart's content. There's plenty of grub here, provided you aren't too hungry. By the way, do you think we'll have much trouble finding Professor Valdmere?"

"Yes, I do. This is a terrible region in which to find your way about. There's no telling where the professor might have gone, although it's reasonable to suppose that he would travel east in the direction of the ranches and settlements. Then, too, there's the possibility that he's been recaptured."

"Don't say that. I had just begun to hope that, perhaps, we were nearing the end of all our troubles. You don't seem very optimistic."

"Well, to tell you the truth, I'm not. If you only knew how diabolical and clever that gang is, you wouldn't wonder at it. They're absolutely ruthless and won't give up until they have achieved their ends."

"But I—I don't understand. What is it they want?"

"Professor Valdmere's secret, I suppose."

"You must be wrong there," retorted Ted. "From

what Miss Valdmere said, the formulas and papers were removed from the safe in the professor's office."

Philo bolted a mouthful of food, took a deep draft from the water bottle before making a reply.

"Perhaps you're right. It's all pretty much of a tangle to me."

Ted's face fell. "Philo," he admonished him, "either you aren't very observing or you are terribly dense. It seems to me you might have picked up a lot of information while you were with the gang. At the very least, I should think the professor would have told you enough to give you an inkling as to what this is all about."

"I never had a chance to talk to Professor Valdmere. Until last night when we made our escape, we were bound and gagged. During the escape we were too busy trying to get away to do much talking. There is only one thing that may help to enlighten you. Last night, while we were running along together, the professor told me:

" 'If you should escape and I don't, will you tell my daughter to go immediately to the bank at Brownsville, open her safety-deposit box, take home the papers I have entrusted to her care and read them carefully.' "

CHAPTER XIV.

A PINTO SHOWS FIGHT.

"Now," said Ted, "tell me all about the gang."

Philo's appetite had been appeased and the two boys sat on the flat surface of a rock overlooking the little depression. Neither one of them remotely resembled the trig and trim young men of two days before. Their clothing was soiled and torn and great hollow circles showed under their eyes. Neither had slept for hours. It was only by the greatest effort of his will that Ted could keep his chin from dropping forward on his chest, his heavy eye-lids open. Philo's weariness showed in the drawling of his voice, the deep lines that had become etched in his forehead.

"First of all," began Philo, "they're Japanese. There are six in the party and they all seem to be well educated and courteous. In all the time we were with them, they never spoke one rough word to us. One might have thought that we were their guests instead of their prisoners, except that we were bound and gagged. But they apologized for being compelled

to resort to such measures. They actually made
us believe that they were sorry that it had to be.
They regretted that they were compelled to use rope
instead of handcuffs and shackles. It was this very
politeness, this commiseration for us, that led the
way to our escape."

"How was that?" asked Ted.

"Well the ropes chafed our wrists and ankles and
they felt so badly about it last night that they removed them, rubbed some sort of ointment over
our chafed skins and posted three guards to watch
us. We waited for our chance and when it came,
we both darted up from our place near the campfire and started away on the run. It was a desperate
chance and we knew it. The guards were armed
and had every opportunity to shoot us down. But
instead of doing that, they hurled themselves at us
in an effort to bring us down. They almost succeeded, too."

"But why didn't they shoot you?"

Philo shook his head. "That's a question I can't
answer. But I know this much. *Professor Valdmere sensed somehow, knew that those three guards
wouldn't fire a shot.*"

Ted's breath caught. "That seems unusual. How
do you explain it?'

"I can't explain it. Just the same, Professor
Valdmere knew. When we were holding a whispered

consultation near the campfire, he told me that I mustn't be afraid, that the Japs wouldn't shoot. I've come to the conclusion that the Japs wouldn't shoot because the Professor was worth more to them alive than dead."

Open-mouthed, Ted gaped at his chum, then rubbed his chin in perplexity.

"That might apply to the professor, but what about you? They wouldn't have any scruples about killing you. You're worth nothing to them either dead or alive."

"True enough. Just the same, I'd like to remind you that, if they took a pot-shot at me, there was always the danger of hitting the professor. My impression is that they were terribly afraid of hurting the professor in any way."

"I wonder why."

"I'm not good at riddles."

Ted half started to his feet. "I think I have it," he explained. "Profesor Valdmere is a very wealthy man and they are planning on holding him for ransom."

Philo laughed sceptically. "That's a wild guess. There's something more to it than that. It goes deeper than that. I'm sure of it."

With unseeing eyes, Ted studied the outlines of the hills along the ragged horizon. His lips were pressed tightly together and he was deeply immersed in thought. Presently he turned his head and spoke again to Philo.

"You're quite right. Ransom hasn't anything to do with it. Whatever their motive is I can't imagine, but I am quite sure that it has something to do with the Atomic Ray."

"That doesn't seem possible either. From what we know of this case, that is, from what Miss Valdmere told us, they are already in possession of the secret. Don't forget that rifled safe."

"I haven't forgotten it," Ted retorted. "But what I was wondering——"

He broke off, his eyes dilating with fear. Coming from some place on the other side of the depression, they could hear the sound of guarded voices, the familiar beat of footsteps. As if moved by a common spring, they bolted to their feet and fled back through the rocks for a distance of perhaps a hundred yards where they dropped panting to their knees.

"Whew!" puffed Philo. "That was a close call! The Japs, as I live!"

However, Philo was mistaken. It was not the Japs at all, but the three Russian's whom Ted had encountered on so many previous occasions. They swarmed down into the depression, howling their delight, showing by their actions that they were more than pleased at finding the pony. Their first impression, no doubt, was that Spitfire, the incorrigible runaway, had come here of his own volition. Next, they discovered that he was tied, whereupon the leader ran up the few feet to the top of the depression and scanned the country around him, a puzzled expression on his face. Then he went back, untied the pony and led him out. While he was doing this, the other two men jumped forward eagerly and picked up the two saddle-packs.

Not until then did Ted notice that the leader carried a club in his hand. The man had a tight grip upon the reins and, to the boy's utter astonishment, he began pounding the fiery little animal about the shoulders and head. The Russian was a powerful man and the blows would have brought an ordinary horse to his knees. But not Spitfire. Spitfire had come from a different breed, a long line of fighting, half-wild ancestors who had not known the meaning of submission. Neither Ted nor Philo had ever heard the shriek of a horse before, but they heard it now. It was a shriek half of fear, half of rage and it re-echoed through the hills, a sound that curdled their blood . Spitfire reared suddenly, lashing out with both front feet. His sharp hooves caught the leader squarely in the chest and face and the man's nerveless fingers released their hold of the reins and he crumpled to the ground.

But Spitfire had not yet won his fight. The

leader's place was immediately taken by the two other Russians who had dropped the saddle-packs and sprung to their friend's aid. Both tried to seize the reins at once and one of them had actually succeeded in accomplishing this somewhat difficult feat, when Spitfire struck again but this time with his teeth, tearing away a large hunk from the shoulder of the man who held him.

Meanwhile Ted and Philo had not been inactive. Seeing their chance, they had come forward on a dead run. Ted, the quicker of the two, was the first to snatch the revolver from the holster of the fallen leader, not a second too soon. One of the two Russians striving to capture Spitfire, suddenly stepped back with a warning cry, his hand streaking toward his gun. But there it faltered, paused, abruptly slid away from the bone handle as his eyes drilled into the gaping hole of the weapon Ted had acquired. A sharp, commanding voice rang out:

"Hands up, both of you, or I'll drill you through! Philo, hurry over and get their revolvers."

In the meantime, Spitfire saw his chance and bolted away toward the valley. He went at a furious rate, heels throwing up little clouds of sand and rock. Ted smiled grimly after him, then turned to his prisoners.

"Well, I guess the score is even now—thanks to the pinto. If I were to pay you back in your own

medicine, I'd tie you up and leave you here in the
hot sun just as you did me."

"Please, monsieur," cried out one of the Russians,
his white lips trembling. "Not that! Mercy,
monsieur!"

"We're not going to tie you up," Ted answered.
"We don't want to kill you. We have a chance to
pay you back in your own coin, but we'll let that
pass."

"What you do then?' the man quavered.

"Send you packing," flamed Ted. "You're going
to get out of this region and stay out. As soon as
your companion here has recovered, you'll proceed
straight east and keep on travelling until you reach
the settlements. And don't ever come back here. If
you do, I won't be responsible for what may happen
to you"

"But we have no food," objected the man

"That's your funeral, not ours. You got into this
scrape, now get out of it. You left us back in the
hills with greater odds against us than there are
against you. At least, you weren't bound hand and
foot. Where's the other horse?"

"Back there in the brush," pointed the man.

"Ted," remonstrated Philo, "give them one of the
saddle-packs. They don't deserve it, but—but——"

At first Ted hotly refused, but as his anger cooled
he saw that it would serve them no good end to

be too harsh in his methods. No matter what their
adversaries might do, it behooved them to play the
game square. No great victory, he suddenly remembered, had ever been achieved by unfair means
or by foul fighting. Philo was right. Nothing could
gainsay that irrefutable fact.

Stooping, he picked up one of the saddle-packs
and handed it to Philo.

"Give it to them," he said. "Perhaps they'll
need it."

The man, who had previously spoken, stepped
back in surprise. His thin, cruel lips twisted into a
smile.

"Thank you, monsieur."

"Please don't mention it," growled Ted.

"Now that monsieur has been so fair to us, we in
turn will show our gratitude. Eet ees without
worry that you may go your way. We shall go ours
as soon as our friend and leader, Monsieur Kerkovitch, has recovered his senses. You may trust us
implicitly."

"Like fun we will," rasped Philo.

"No," agreed Ted, "we wouldn't trust you out
of our sight. We'll stay right here with you until
you are all in a position to travel. Do you understand?"

"We understand," answered the Russian, suddenly averting his eyes.

CHAPTER XV.

ARMED.

WHILE they were waiting for Kerkovitch to recover consciousness, in the hope that they might discover something that would throw a light on the mystery, Ted and Philo searched the pockets of the three Russians. However, except for a few letters written in Slavic, they found nothing. Retaining the letters for further reference, Ted turned upon the man with whom he had formerly conversed.

"What business have you with Professor Valdmere?" he inquired pointedly.

The person addressed looked at him curiously for a full minute, then broke into a grating laugh.

"That, monsieur, is something I can not tell you."

Ted tried a new tack. "When did you first hear of the Atomic Ray?"

The Russian laughed again. "Eet ees no use, monsieur. We know nothing. Like soldiers we go only when and where we are commanded."

Whereupon Ted lapsed into silence. He could see that he was wasting his breath in attempting to get any information from this source. Yet, once again he turned to the Russian spokesman.

"Kerkovitch certainly made a very serious mistake when he commenced to beat up the horse. Of course, you are under no obligation to tell me the reason if you do not wish to do so, but I would be very much interested to know why he did it. He must have a savage temper. Just because he was unsuccessful in his other quest, is no reason why he should vent his wrath upon a poor, dumb beast."

The Russian, apparently, had no scruples in supplying his interrogator with this information. He grinned amusedly.

"Kerkovitch ees very angry with that horse. After we leave you yesterday, he ride upon that horse feeling very glad that he not have to walk any more. But no sooner he think that, when the pony jump very quick and Kerkovitch find himself sitting on the rocks. The horse run away, but monsieur, our leader, was shaken up and hurt very badly and he became very angry. He told us that if he ever saw that horse again he would kill him."

"The horse meant no harm," said Philo. "No doubt, he was frightened. Anyone who takes out his anger on a dumb animal has no sense of decency at all. I'm glad now that Kerkovitch received his just dues."

The person under discussion, moaned, raised a

limp hand and soon afterward recovered consciousness. Soon he was sitting up, staring dazedly about
him. When his glance met those of the two boys,
he started visibly as if he had seen an apparition.
His right hand went to his holster—but there was
no gun there.

"Thought you'd seen a ghost, eh?" Ted could
not repress the note of triumph in his voice. "Well,
the tables are turned, Mr. Kerkovitch. How do
you like it?"

The leader's answer was not intelligible. He
stumbled to his feet, snarling something under his
breath. Groaning, his hand went up to his injured,
crushed jaw. Ted's gaze followed the movement.

"That ought' to teach you a lesson," he declared.
"If you hadn't tried to beat up that poor pony with
a club, you might still be in possession of a whole
skin."

The Russian broke into a wild torrent of abuse
directed at Ted and the pony.

"Thees affair ees not finished yet," he stormed.
"Remember what I told you last time. Well, I
repeat it, monsieur. Alex Kerkovitch neither forgets
nor forgives. Some day you will be very sorry."

Ted laughed coldly. "All that may be very true,
Mr. Kerkovitch, but just now you'll have to admit
that we have the upper hand."

"Tomorrow or the next day the situation may be different," hinted the aggrieved man.

"You won't be around here tomorrow—or next week either. You're starting for the settlements right away. We're going to see you keep on moving. Your life won't be worth a plugged nickle if you come back."

Although the Russian did not know what a plugged nickle was, he understood Ted's meaning perfectly.

"You mean we go back to Langdon Pairie?" he asked.

"If you like. You can exercise your own prerogative. All I'm asking is that you don't come back here."

The injured leader started to protest but Ted cut him short.

"Enough of that!" he threatened, flourishing the gun. "March!"

Down through the rocks, straight into the path of the burning morning sunlight the disgruntled trio made their way, standing arm-in-arm, the two boys watched them go, feeling that at least one menace had been removed, one danger averted. They were confident that they would not be troubld by the Russians again.

"Thank goodness, that's over," Philo breathed a sigh of relief. "We got out of this scrape pretty lucky. When this affair is all over, one of the first things I think we ought to do it to erect a monument to your outlaw pony, Spitfire. Miss Valdmere showed a lot of good judgment when she bought that horse."

Ted laughed. "Wonder where he is now. I don't suppose he'll stop until he reaches Brent's camp. Well, let's get the other pony and turn him loose, too. He can graze about or return with Spitfire. We haven't any use for a pony now."

To this Philo readily agreed. The morning was well advanced and as yet they had done nothing in the missing man's behalf. If they did not find Professor Valdmere soon, the chances were they might not find him at all. For, as Philo pointed out, the Japs were engaged in the same quest.

"They outnumber us," he concluded, "so the odds are in their favor. While we've been fooling our time away with these Russians, they've probably succeeded in discovering some trace of him."

"I wouldn't say that we've wasted our time," Ted pointed out. "We have weapons now—and that is something. We'll be in much better position to meet Professor Valdmere's enemies."

"Yes, that's true."

"Where would you suggest to search first?" asked Ted.

Philo puckered his lips and scowled lightly.

"To tell you the honest truth, I don't know. It's all guesswork. If something hasn't happened to him, he ought to be as far east as we are now. He's a strong, robust man and would certainly travel as fast as I did. He'll be in this vicinity somewhere unless——" Philo paused, scratching his head.

"I know what you were going to say," Ted took up the sentence where his chum had left off. "You were intending to point out that Professor Valdmere could not be very far away unless one of two things have happened. That he's been recaptured by the Japs, or that he's searching around in the hills for you."

"You can set your mind to rest on that last score," said Philo thoughtfully.

"What makes you say that? Are you so sure the Japs have captured him?"

The other nodded his head gloomily. One shouldn't be a pessimist, but I have that feeling. I really believe that that gang not only have retaken Professor Valdmere but that my own escape was not so much a matter of luck as it was of intention."

"I don't understand you."

Philo smiled mysteriously. "Sounds queer, doesn't it? I might have put it in a different way. The Japs don't want to bother with small fry like me They're out after bigger game."

"I'm beginning to get an inkling of what you

mean," Ted's face lighted with sudden comprehension. He leaned forward and grasped his chum's arm tightly.

"They didn't care much whether you escaped or not."

"That's it exactly. I'm harmless as a babe. What chance have I against six armed men?"

"Then you think we ought to go over to the place where the Japs were camped last night and see if the Professor is there?"

Philo nodded his head emphatically. "Our logical course under the circumstances. At any rate, it will do away with all this guesswork. If Professor Valdmere is not there, so much the better. We'll know then that he's making his way eastward—and to safety. We won't need to worry any more,"

"Unless he could happen to fall in with those Russians," grimaced Ted.

It was evident that such a contingeny had not occurred to Philo, judging from the startled expression that had suddenly leaped into his eyes.

"Good Heavens!"

"Let us hope that he doesn't," Ted hurried on. "The probability is that he wouldn't ever see them. But enough of this. Are you ready to start?"

Each carrying a saddle-pack, they set out in the direction of the valley, into which they descended a few minutes later. Philo in the lead, they crossed the valley floor, stubbornly negotiated the opposite slope and soon were wending their way through a country of forbidding appearance. The sun flamed down upon them with an oppressive, malignant glare. Reserving their full strength for the physical effort before them, they spoke only when absolutely necessary and then only in sleepy monosyllables.

On and on, the road seemed interminable to Ted, who actually half slept on the perpendicular. To his ears the monotonous beat of their footsteps became a sort of weird, half-musical cadence, beating into his sleep-weary brain. Thus he was not prepared, only dimly realized what Philo meant when his chum's hand was abruptly flung to his arm, forcibly pulling him down.

"Great Scott, are you half cuckoo—or what? Quick now—slip down behind this rock!"

CHAPTER XVI.

THE BOYS MEET A STRANGER.

THERE was really no need for caution, however, as events subsequently proved. When the person Philo had heard came into view, the two boys jumped to their feet. They had never seen him before but right away his appearance struck and held their attention. Without fear, they advanced toward him. Perceiving them, the man stopped short.

"Hello!" he cried out in surprise. "Where did you fellows come from?"

"We might ask you the same question," Ted grinned as he and Philo advanced closer to the stranger. "We saw by your headgear that you're a pilot. But where is your plane?"

The man's face grew instantly sober.

"Unfortunately I'm not the piilot," he answered. "That's where the difficulty comes in. I'm only a passenger and my pilot was taken suddenly ill enroute. We were forced to land here in this awful wilderness. Sturgis—he's the pilot—circled around until he discovered a shack, which looked as though

it might be inhabited. There was a fairly level place
nearby and we made the landing.   But before the
plane taxied to a stop, Sturgis was unconscious.   I
pulled him out of the front cockpit and carried him
up to the house, thinking, of course, that there were
people there."

"And you found it deserted?" Philo's voice could
not conceal the interest he felt.

The former airplane passenger stared at them a
little wildly.

"But it was inhabited.   Bears!"

"Bears!" exclaimed the two boys in unison.

"Three of 'em!" the stranger moistened his lips.
"A mother and two cubs. Didn't see them until I
got right in. Door was open, you know, and I thought
the owner of the place had stepped out somewhere
for a few minutes and——"

"They attacked you," guessed Philo, his eyes wide.

"A wild scramble, if you know what I mean,"
the man's face clouded with the memory. "I was at
a disadvantage with Sturgis in my arms. I couldn't
move very rapidly.   Still, it is surprising what a man
can do in—in an emergency like that. I succeeded in
getting on top of the table, the mother bear cuffing at
me and growling something terrible. The cubs raced
through the door but that old she devil tipped over
the table before she condescended to leave. I landed
in a corner, the limp body of Sturgis on top of me.

I tell you it was awful. For a time I thought it was all over for both of us."

"You were lucky to get out of it as easily as you did," Ted consoled him.

"Well, I should say so. Nothing but a bad scare and this lump on my head." The stranger paused to show it to them. "But there was a bunk there without blankets and—and—I put Sturgis on it. By that time I had begun to notice how bare and dirty the place looked. It suddenly came over me that it had been unoccupied for months. Investigation proved that I was right. No food, water—nothing! Terrible predicament! For a time, I think, I nearly went out of my head. I didn't care so much for myself—but there was Sturgis, as fine a chap as I've ever met, desperately ill, and I couldn't even fly the plane."

"What is your name?" asked Ted.

"George Evanson. My home is in Los Angeles."

"I can't imagine how you felt," sympathized Philo. "Is this er—Mr. Sturgis dead?"

"No, but he will be if we don't get help to him soon. You boys are acquainted around here. Can you tell me where I'd be apt to find a doctor or a trained nurse. Where is the nearest house or telephone?"

The two boys exchanged a quick look of dismay, while Ted's cheeks slowly paled.

"There aren't any," he replied.

"No houses, you mean?"   The stranger's lips quivered.

"Terrible as it may seem, that's the truth.   Not a house or telephone within thirty miles.   No food either, except what we have in these saddle-packs."

The man mumbled something under his breath and sat down on a rock, putting his head in his hands.   His shoulders heaved with suppressed emotion.   Again Ted and Philo exchanged glances.

"You'll have to do it, Ted," said Philo with sudden decision.   "You must, Ted—you must try.   Mr. Evanson ought to be willing to take your place in our search for Professor Valdmere if—if you do that."

The stranger raised his head suddenly and stared at Philo.

"Do what?" he demanded. "What do you mean?"

"Fly to Langdon Prairie," came the prompt answer.

The man's mouth gaped open.   "You—you mean this boy here, this—this young friend of yours, knows how to operate an airplane?"

"He does," Philo nodded his head.   "You see, we both work for the Northern Airplane Corporation at Minneapolis.   He's been up several times alone."

"I'm not an experienced flyer," put in Ted modestly, "but with luck I might make it."

The stranger popped to his feet, exclaiming wildly, and threw one arm about Ted's waist.

"Boy, you gotta do it!" he shouted. "Think of that poor devil lying there all alone. He'll die unless help comes. Tell me you'll do it. It would be criminal to leave him there if you know the first thing about flying."

"I'll try, of course," Ted reassured him. "But you'll have to help out, too. The work in which we're engaged is probably even more important than getting this pilot, Sturgis, to the hospital."

"What is this work?"

"While you're leading the way to the place where your friend is, I'll tell you. How far is that shack from here?"

"I'm not sure. About two miles, I should estimate." The stranger turned as he spoke, motioning for them to follow. "Up through some hills, then a sort of plateau, fairly level, at the far end of which you'll find the cabin. The machine is close by." He pressed closer to Ted. "How about this work you mentioned?"

"You've heard of Professor Valdmere, I suppose?"

"Certainly," smiled the man. "Who hasn't?"

"Well, he's up here in the hills somewhere, trying to escape from a party of desperate criminals—all of whom are Japanese. There's been a serious plot directed against him. He was taken from his place at Brownsville early yesterday morning."

Evanson stopped short. He looked squarely into Ted's eyes.

"That's absurd!" he exclaimed. "You don't mean it."

"I do mean it. The first demonstration of Professor Valdmere never took place. Didn't the news come over the wire to Missoula?"

"There was some news but nothing like that. The papers carried a story, believed to be authentic—it came over the United Press' leased wire—that the scientist was ill and had postponed the first demonstrations, which should have taken place yesterday."

"Who gave out that statement?" gasped Ted.

"Valdmere's private secretary, I believe. At any rate, someone met the reporters at the gate and gave out that information. No one, of course, was permitted on the grounds and naturally there was no chance to verify anything."

"The plot goes much deeper than I had supposed," mused Ted. "Imagine that gang carrying off things in that high-handed manner. But I'll give you my word that Professor Valdmere is here."

"Then there won't be a demonstration of the Atomic Ray at all?"

"Certainly not—unless the Professor is found. What makes you think there will be?"

"Well, the papers said there would."

"Imagine such nonsense," sniffed Philo. "What do the papers know about it? I suppose the private secretary gave out that information, too."

"That's exactly what he did," the stranger nodded his head. "That's why I'm here. I paid Sturgis fifty dollars to bring me over. If he hadn't taken unexpectedly ill, I'd be in Brownsville this very minute."

"And a lot of good it would have done you," Ted pointed out. "Professor Valdmere can't be in two places at once."

The stranger laughed. "True enough. But are you quite sure he's here?"

"Certainly we're sure," Ted retorted angrily.

"Can you swear to it?"

Ted was cornered. He commenced to stammer and hesitate, looking beseechingly at his chum.

"Ted can't swear to it but I can," Philo told the doubting Mr. Evanson. "Up until a few hours ago, I was with Professor Valdmere. We were both held prisoners."

"But how do you know it was Professor Valdmere?" persisted the man. "I'm not doubting your word, you understand. I'm merely seeking information. You've just said you were with Professor Valdmere. Are you sure you could identify him?"

"Yes."

"How?"

"By his resemblance to the pictures I've seen of him."

"That isn't conclusive, of course. Just the same, I'm now inclined to believe that the person you were with *is* Professor Valdmere, and that the other is an imposter."

Both Ted and Philo started visibly. Was this man absolutely crazy—or what?

"Sa—say," gurgled Ted, "what do you mean by that? Imposter! I don't understand. Who is this other person you speak of?"

"I wish I could tell you," said the man, "but I can't. It's all very bewildering. You will appreciate this when I tell you that a picture was taken yesterday afternoon at Brownsville of a person said to be Professor Valdmere and telegraphed to every part of the United States. That picture was taken by some reporter standing outside the fence of the scientist's estate and——" Evanson paused, coughing.

"Yes, yes—go on!" cried both boys in one voice.

"And the person photographed," concluded the stranger, "whether you believe it or not, is the dead image of Professor Valdmere!"

CHAPTER XVII.

WHAT THE "LANCET" TOLD

STARTLING, indeed, was this information. Complicated and seemingly unsolvable before, the mystery surrounding Professor Valdmere had become even more complex. If this stranger spoke the truth—and there was no reason just then to doubt his word—what did it all mean? What were the motives underlying all the inexplicable events that had taken place since yesterday morning? It was no ordinary plot. There seemed to be no rhyme nor reason in anything. One grew bewildered and perplexed trying to puzzle it all out. This new development had so completely taken the two boys by surprise that for the remainder of the journey to the lone cabin where the pilot, Sturgis, lay helpless, neither had a great deal to say.

When Philo and Mr. Evanson went within to ascertain how the aviator had fared in the latter's absence, Ted walked over to the plane and began to examine it. It was a foreign-made steel plane, into which had been set a high-powered motor of a type then very popular in Europe. It was this fact which first tended to arouse a faint glimmer of suspicion in the mind of the young aviator. Even though he accepted the improbable story Evanson had told, it was a little hard to account for the fact that Sturgis, an American airman, had come into possesssion of a foreign machine. Local pilots had been trained to use American planes and it was seldom that a machine like this was to be found in common use in the United States.

Ted paused for a moment to reflect. Suddenly through his mind there leaped a disconcerting premonition. If Sturgis was a commercial aviator, why did he not use an American airplane? Owing to the difficulty of securing parts for the motor in this country, it would be very costly to operate.

Notwithstanding, the plane was a good one and Ted's critical eye ran over her trim lines with approval. The controls were a little unfamiliar to him and, acting almost subconsciously, he clambered into the front cockpit and began experimenting with the levers. Next he went over the motor carefully, finding it to be in good working order. The fuel tank was large and the indicator showed that he had enough gas to last for three or four hundred miles.

"Sturgis must be an aristocratic barn-stormer," he mused. "I'll bet this monoplane didn't cost him less than fifteen thousand dollars. She's a beauty and no mistake. Just the same, before we fly her, I'm going to have a confidential little chat with the alleged Mr. Evanson. How do I know he isn't in the employ of the Japs? Also how do I know that Sturgis is really ill? This may be only another attempt on the part of that gang, or some other crowd like the Russians, to work injury to the cause of Professor Valdmere.

Indeed, the more he thought about it, the more suspicious he became. To begin with, Evanson's story seemed a bit too far fetched. One must be credulous to swallow it. Two men posing as Professor Valdmere. Ridiculous! Even a child would hesitate before giving such a story credence.

At this juncture, an object in the rear cockpit caught his attention. There was a gleam of sun against something white and, as his eyes focused upon it, he perceived that it was the folded copy of a newspaper. Instantly he turned, scrambled into the rear cockpit, his pulses throbbing in his wrists like two tiny hearts.

His excitement grew as he noted the date line— June 24th! His eyes seemed to blur and his fingers fluttered so badly that it was all he could do to complete the task of unfolding the paper. It was a breathless moment, fraught with possibilities. In a few seconds now he would know beyond any shadow of a doubt whether Evanson's strange tale were true or false.

His eyes nearly popped from his head as he saw that the name of the paper, printed in block letters at the top of the page, was the Missoula *Lancet*. Thus far Evanson's queer story had been corroborated. Now for the article and the photograph of the man who resembled Professor Valdmere! Ted could scarcely contain himself. He was in such a hurry to trace this thing to its ultimate end that, in turning the sheet in his hand, the wind flipped back one of the pages, ripping off a corner. Another wisp of breeze came at this juncture and the fated purveyor of news tore itself spitefully out of the other hand, glided along the dope covering the fuselage, then, with almost human ingenuity, spread itself out like a sail, bellying and fluttering and soaring in the next vagrant breeze. By the time Ted had jumped out of the plane in hot pursuit, the door of the cabin swung open and Evanson and Philo emerged. Paying not the slightest attention to them, Ted raced across the yard, hurdled a four-foot-high rock pile and literally drove through the air to complete a flying tackle of the elusive *Lancet*. Ted, of course, did not feel that the effort was wasted, but to two innocent onlookers like Evanson and Philo, his queer antics produced an unexpected effect.

The latter emitted an astonished little gasp and

sat down upon the nearest flat rock, absolutely sure in his own mind that his chum had suddenly taken leave of his senses. Evanson also looked mildly startled and paused in wonder.

Meanwhile Ted's gaze fairly froze over the front page and in that tense, desperate look he seemed to be seeing every article and headline at once. And —low and behold!—here again came the unexpected. Evanson had not lied at all. Impressed before his eyes, clear-cut down to the last detail, was the photograph of Professor Valdmere's double—*if not Professor Valdmere himself.*

CHAPTER XVIII.

A YOUNG PILOT TAKES THE AIR.

"In the name of common sense," gasped Philo, "have you gone completely cookoo? Ted, what is the matter with you? We thought you were examining the plane, but instead of that, here you are performing around the yard like an escaped lunatic."

Then and there, Ted decided that it would never do for him to tell what had been going on in his mind. His suspicions in regard to Evanson had proved to be absolutely without foundation. The story he had told, incredible as it had seemed, had been verified by the picture in the *Lancet*. It was all so strange and bewildering that it was hard to know what to think—or what to do. He turned sheepishly toward his two companions.

"I don't see that there is anything so unusual about my actions," he defended himself. This newspaper is the one that has the picture of the man claimed to be Professor Valdmere. I was looking at it over near the plane when the wind whipped it out of my hand. I think it must be the paper you left there,

Mr. Evanson," Ted concluded, handing it over to its rightful owner. "I found it in the rear cockpit."

"So it is," Evanson's face brightened. "I'd forgotten all about it. Must have had it in my hand when we took off at the Missoula flying field. Well, I'm glad you happened to find it. It will verify everything I've told you and will also explain how it came about that I set out on this trip."

"How's Sturgis?" asked Ted.

"In terrible pain," Philo answered. "And you must hurry, Ted. Think you can fly that plane?"

"It's not very familiar to me," Ted admitted, "but I'm willing to try. "You see——" turning upon Mr. Evanson—"it's a foreign machine and the controls aren't what I'm used to. I've been wondering how Sturgis could afford to own a plane like that."

"It isn't his," answered Evanson. "The machine Sturgis usually operates is in a hanger in Missoula undergoing some repairs. This plane was rented for the occasion from some other person."

"For Sturgis' sake, I'm going to fly it. If everything goes well, I'll have him in the hospital in Langdon Prairie in less than an hour. While you fellows are bringing Sturgis out, I'll tune up."

Hurrying back to the plane, Ted began warming up the motor. His eyes sparkled as he listened to its strumming, steady roar. To be sure that everything was in apple-pie order, he went over the machine carefully, even pausing to examine the flying wires and empennage. By the time he had finished, Philo and Evanson arrived from the house, carrying the unconscious pilot. He assisted them in placing the man in a comfortable position in the rear cockpit. When this was done, he clambered into his seat, shouting out to his two companions.

"Stand back, now. I'm taking off. Good-bye."

Their answering shouts were drowned in the roar of the machine as he threw the stick forward and taxied and bumped along the rough plateau. In a moment he had attained flying speed and was zooming skyward like a rocket, his nervousness gone.

"She's a beauty," he exclaimed enthusiastically to himself, glorying in this thrill of a perfect machine performing like clock-work under him. It was the first plane of this type that he had ever driven. She handled perfectly, responding to his will like a thing of life. Nose pointing upward, he made altitude, so it seemed to him, with the swiftness of an arrow. Rocks, trees, hills—everything was dropping away from under with the speed of a falling express elevator. The cabin, near which he had taken off, was now only a tiny speck indented against the gray-brown carpet of the earth.

Plane on a level keel, now that he had attained altiture, he winged his way eastward in the general direction of Langdon Pairie. Becoming more accustomed to his controls, he had plenty of time for reflection. For the first time, it occurred to him that with this airplane in his possession, he was in a much better position to find Professor Valdmere than at any time since that memorable morning ·in Brownsville, two days ago.

The air up here above the earth was tonic and invigorating and he found himself laying plans, following the twisting threads of his past experiences in an effort to solve the mystery. Forced to accept the fact of another person at Brownsville whom the public had accepted as the real Professor Valdmere, he endeavored, though not with a great deal of success, to figure out his identity.

Of one thing, however, he was sure—and that was that the real Professor Valdmere was the one they had been following and not the person who had posed for the photograph which subsequently had appeared in the press. Assuming that this was the case, who then was the imposter? Why had the conspirators brought him to Brownsville?

Debating these questions pro and con, Ted presently decided that the case was too complex for him. The nearest approach to a satisfactory solution was that the second Professor Valdmere had been introduced in an effort on the part of the conspirators to keep the public in complete ignorance of what was going on. Working from this hypothesis, one was led to another somewhat startling conclusion: that the members of the strange gang working against the famous scientist had not yet been wholly successful in achieving their ends. In other words, there remained something yet to be done.

Ted puckered his brow thoughtfully, gazing out over the nose of his speeding plane. Why was everything wrapped in that concealing cloak of mystery and intrigue? One could take nothing for granted. Unless one had absolute proof of things, how was he to know what was true and what was false, pick and choose from among the tangled threads of the inexplicable plot?

Suddenly he started as his mind gave space for a disconcerting thought. For all he knew, Miss Valdmere herself, might be other than what she seemed, the daughter of the real Professor Valdmere. He actually trembled all over as the realization left its startling impress. Miss Valdmere herself a traitor—one of the gang! Could it be? Until that morning in Brownsville he had never seen the girl. Come to think of it, he couldn't recall that he had ever read anywhere that the great scientist had a daughter.

For a full minute, he sat staring out into space, his heart troubled. Then his expression brightened and he broke into a joyous peal of laughter. What a fool he was! Imagine suspecting little Miss Valdmere—of all persons. Why, it was ridiculous. Philo would be the next to come under suspicion, if he kept on at this rate, he told himself.

The mind has a curious method all its own at arriving at results. Every thought is correlated with some other thought and in the brain processes new ideas are manufactured every minute. Thinking of Miss Valdmere had given Ted a lead. It had popped into his head apparently from nowhere. It was that, inasmuch as Miss Valdmere was the real daughter of the real scientist, she would know her own father. The public might be fooled by that photograph of a rank imposter, but not the girl. She would detect the imposition at once.

"Now," thought Ted, "just as soon as I have taken Sturgis to the hospital, I'll turn right around and fly back to the place where Miss Peggy is and pick her up. Then we'll both go on and join Mr. Evanson and Philo. I'll show her that photograph and get her opinion of it. That will settle the matter of these two professors for all time."

Thinking of these things, he slipped down to a lower elevation to get his bearings. Though he couldn't see Langdon Prairie yet, he knew that he couldn't have very much farther to go. He had left the hills far behind. The topography of the earth below him indicated that he was flying over a level stretch of country—the prairie he and Miss

Valdmere had crossed the day before. If he could look down and discover a faint, threadlike path etched across the level plain, he could be assured that it was the Hills Road.

But such a path was nowhere to be seen. Fearful at last that he was off his course entirely, he began circling around, widening his arc with each revolution. At the end of fifteen minutes, he had occasion to compliment himself upon the wisdom of this manœuvre, for, unexpectedly, off to his right he perceived not the road but the town itself.

The inference was that he had charted his course too far to the north and had actually passed the town without seeing it. Grinning over this error in his reckoning, he swerved sharply and began winging his way straight for his goal. In less than ten minutes, he had picked out his landing place in an unobstructed field just outside the town and was gliding to earth. Almost before he was aware, the big plane was sweeping along a level runway, taxiing slower and slower until she had come to a full stop.

Cheeks slightly pale as a result of his nervousness in bringing his unfamiliar craft safely to earth, Ted unbuckled his safety strap and rose and looked about him.

CHAPTER XIX

FORCED LANDING

AN airplane is an uncommon sight in Langdon Prairie, a fact which Ted had wholly overlooked, and which reacted to his benefit shortly after his arrival. Within a few minutes of the time he had stepped out of the cockpit with the intention of making his way over the village to secure help in removing the body of Sturgis, an automobile turned off the main road and made its way toward him.

The driver of the car threw on his brake and paused directly opposite.

"Hello, stranger," he called out. "Are you in trouble?"

"Yes," answered Ted, quick to seize upon this opportunity. "I have a man here with me who is seriously ill and must be taken to the hospital. Will you help me?"

By way of answer, the driver jumped out of the car and hurried forward.

"What you want me to do?" he asked.

"Assist me to get my friend, Mr. Sturgis, out

of the plane and into your car. It's very important that he should have medical attention at once."

With true western spirit, the driver rolled up his sleeves and he and Ted set to work. Barely had they raised Sturgis' limp body from the cockpit when Ted heard the sound of other cars and in an incredible short time they were surrounded by a gaping, inquisitive crowd.

Now, it had been Ted's intention to accompany Sturgis to the hospital, but with the coming of the crowd he saw that this would never do. No telling what might happen to the plane in his absence with all these people hanging around. On the other hand, it didn't look just right to run away without first ascertaining that the pilot would be properly cared for. In a moment of inspiration, he explained his predicament to the man who was helping him.

"Don't you worry about that," the other quickly reassured him. "I got friends here in the crowd that can help me take this man down to the hospital. I give you my word that he'll be looked after the same as if he was my own brother. So you feel that you ought to hurry back to them folks out there?"

"Yes, it is very important. It may be a matter of life and death. But how can I ever thank you?"

By this time he had made Sturgis comfortable in

the back seat of the stranger's automobile. They paused to shake hands.

"You don't need to thank me," said the man. "It's all right. Good luck to you."

Greatly relieved, Ted turned back and clambered again to his place in the cockpit. Before warming up, he was forced to motion back the crowd which was pressing in on him from every side. This task accomplished, he soon had the motor working and, a few minutes later, the crowd cheering him, he taxied down the field and took the air.

"Thank goodness, that's over," he sighed relievedly. "So far, so good. Now if I can only find Miss Valdmere."

Half an hour afterward he had located the chuck-wagon but the topography of the country, he observed, would make it very difficult to land his plane. A more experienced pilot might not have hesitated but Ted, who had handled a plane only a few times alone dreaded to think of what might happen should he make the attempt. The slightest mistake on his part would send him crashing into the rocks.

Time and time again, he wheeled and came back, flying the carpet, then rising again to safer altitude. To make the situation doubly perilous, a strong wind was now sweeping over the range and the air was filling with pockets. An unexpected bump sent him into a half-roll and he emerged safely from this only to discover that he had driven into a bank of mist and could see nothing.

Thereafter, one misfortune followed another. Plowing up through the mists, he reached an area unaffected by storm, but had lost his bearings. Down below were no landmarks to guide him, nothing but a dreary, treacherous stretch of rain clouds, flying low and obscuring the earth. He marked the course of these clouds in an effort to get his directions. At a lower altitude the wind had been blowing from the northwest. These flying clouds, therefore, must be moving southeast. He turned and began to follow them.

"It's only a squall and it'll blow over in a few minutes," he tried to comfort himself. "If I keep up here for a while, I can go back and make that landing yet."

At heart, however, Ted was not as optimistic as he would try to make himself believe. For all he knew, the storm might not abate before night. He couldn't keep on flying indefinitely and it would be difficult to land. The situation was not one he cared to dwell upon.

While he was trying to decide what ought to be done, the matter was taken completely out of his hands by the plane itself. Unexpectedly the motor conked and he was forced into a glide. It was terrifying at first but after that a strange calmness possessed him. If he could keep his machine under control he could plane to earth with reasonable assurance that he was east of the range of hills and would alight on the level prairie.

Owing to the fact that his craft was a cabin plane, fitted up with air-tight compartments, three windows on each side, there was very little visibility with the rain beating around him and dense clouds of mist rolling up before a violent wind. The glass shield in front dripped with water and even by crouching close behind it he could see very little, was not sure, when an opaque body came up to meet him, whether it was earth or cloud. As he neared it, breathing a fervent hope that it was land, he pulled back the control stick and shut his eyes.

But there was no crash. He made a ground loop, however, in trying to avoid an obstruction close at hand, then came to a jarring stop.

It had been a close call and a surge of elation and thankfulness went through him. Now that it was all over, the reaction had set in, leaving him weak and dizzy. Relaxing in his seat, he kept repeating over and over again.

"I'm glad! I'm glad! I'm glad!"

The wind and the rain were still driving furiously and he was more than pleased that he was sheltered here in the cabin instead of sitting in an open cockpit. He devoutly hoped that in making his landing

he had not injured the plane. He was not particularly perturbed over the fact that he had had trouble
with his motor. When it stopped raining, he was
sure that he would soon have it working again.

He began wondering vaguely where he was. One
thing that puzzled him was that he had landed close
to the hill range. His course had been southeast
up to the time his motor had conked and, according
to his reckoning, he should have been miles east of
the range in level, open country. But while he was
pondering over this, the solution came to him. He
remembered now that instead of running directly
north and south, the range swung away at its
southern end, making a sort of loop. The end of
this loop came to within a few miles of Brownsville
and could be seen distinctly from Professor Valdmere's estate.

Once more reassured, he settled back in his seat,
smiling to himself. When the storm subsided, it
wouldn't take him long to get back to the vicinity
of the chuck-wagon—and Miss Valdmere. This time,
instead of trying to land on the little hog's back
upon which Brent had camped, he'd make his landing in a more level place, not far from the spot
where they had abandoned the car. After his experiences of that fateful afternoon, he didn't propose to take any more chances. It would be much
better to walk from the vicinity of the car to the

chuck-wagon than to risk everything in a difficult, hazardous landing.

Exactly at five o'clock the rain ceased. The wind had abated, too, with the promise of clear weather for the return trip. He had got out and had been working on the motor for less than a quarter of an hour, when the sun itself, flaming across the world, touched the hills and prairie with golden, glorious magic.

Nothing could have cheered him up quite so much as that change from darkling storm to clear skies and sunlight. He actually commenced to whistle as he completed his work on the motor and began testing his controls. Afterward he warmed up his machine, watching his oil gauge to see that his oil-line was working properly, then, with more confidence than he had felt since taking charge of the big monoplane, he taxied along the ground and took the air.

Climbing swiftly, he gave her the gun, a feeling of exultation upon him. Visibility was wonderful now and he was quite sure that he would have no trouble in finding Brent's camp. As a matter of fact, he picked up the trail from Langdon Prairie within twenty minutes of his take-off and in another ten minutes he had executed a left-bank, turned nose down and planed for an open field between two sheltering hills.

He had landed less than a hundred yards from the trail and two hundred yards from Miss Valdmere's stalled automobile. He came out of the cockpit, grinning, a pail in his hand. Fate had played him a scurvy trick the other day when they had run out of gasoline, but he was confident that he could turn the tables now. Laughing, he drained out a full gallon of precious liquid from the monoplane's large tank and hurried down to the car.

"Maybe this is borrowing from Peter to pay Paul," he smiled to himself, "but I don't think anyone is going to object."

Altogether there was a good deal of satisfaction in this ruse and Ted felt highly elated with himself. Plumping down in the front seat of the car, behind the wheel, he switched on the juice, set his foot confidently upon the starter and the thrumming under him told him that his efforts had not been in vain.

A moment later, he threw in the clutch and started up the hill.

"Miss Valdmere will be surprised to see me," he grinned.

CHAPTER XX

THE SEARCH BEGINS ANEW.

IF Ted had expected that Miss Valdmere would be surprised to see him, his expectations were fulfilled. With a cry that was almost a sob she sprang toward him and in the excitement of the moment actually threw her arms about his neck.

"Why Ted Winters," she choked, "where—where —why, it's really you."

Her tears were falling and for the embarrassed young man the situation was a little difficult. He had never had a sister of his own and was not at all familiar with the idiosyncrasies of girls.

"There! There!" he patted her arm. "It's quite all right. I've come to get you, Miss Peggy—and— and we'll go and find your father; that is if you can get away. Are you all alone here?"

Miss Valdmere dried her eyes, which were shining like two stars. She sobbed once or twice more out of pure happiness. Then she discovered that her arms were where they shouldn't have been, and she removed them with a startled jerk, flushing furiously.

"Ted, I didn't mean th—that," she stammered. "I—I—the action was entirely involuntary."

"Of course, it was," said Ted, horribly embarrassed himself. "I know how you must feel. It's all right, Miss Valdmere."

"Did you meet the posse?" she asked.

"Posse!" Ted looked at her in surprise.

"Yes, don't you remember that Mr. Brent told you that night when we separated that he would take me back here and then hurry on to the Circle W Ranch to get help?"

Ted nodded his head. "I remember now."

"He did just what he said he would," continued Miss Valdmere. "It was late when we got back here to the chuck-wagon. He must have been nearly as tired as I was but he wouldn't stop. He got us something to eat and then right afterward he set out. It is twelve miles over to the ranch and he walked every step of the way, routed them all out of bed and, under the direction of his friend, Mr. Strebbing, they formed a posse of eight, armed themselves with revolvers and rifles and were back here before I woke up. They brought a woman with them, Mr. Strebbing's mother, to keep me company. I was glad, because it is terribly lonesome here."

"Where's Mrs. Strebbing now?" asked Ted, looking about him.

"She's over in the chuck-wagon. Come with me

and I'll introduce you. But first I want to know if you have any news from Father."

"Only that he has escaped from that party of Japanese," Ted informed her.

She clapped her hands in delight.

"Oh, Ted, tell me you're not joking. Have you seen him? Did you talk to him? What did he say?"

"No, I haven't seen him. He and Philo escaped last night. During their flight—you see, they were pursued by the Japanese—your father and Philo became separated, went in different directions. By sheer luck, more than anything else, I found Philo in a little valley about forty miles from here. Quite early this morning it was. I won't bother you with all the details, because I really haven't the time. Philo and a man named Evanson are out looking for your father now. I'm hoping that they'll find him before night."

"So do I. But I don't quite understand, Ted, how you got here so soon."

"That's a long story, Miss Peggy. Some very unusual things have happened since I saw you last. I've been to Langdon Pairie in an airplane and—"

"Ted Winters, what are you talking about?"

"It's true. I took Mr. Evanson's pilot to the hospital this afternoon. You see, he became suddenly ill and was compelled to make a forced landing up there in the hills. On my return I though I'd pick you up, but I ran into a storm and was forced back almost to Brownsville."

The girl continued to stare at Ted, wonder still in her eyes.

"Were you in that airplane that was circling around here above our heads just before that storm?" she demanded.

Ted nodded. "Correct, Miss Peggy. I didn't land, though, because I was afraid. The field is narrow here, giving a flyer very little chance. While I was wondering what I ought to do, the storm hit me—clouds so dense and the rain so furious that there was no visibility. I mean by that that I couldn't see anything. To save my own skin, I had to make altitude, try to get above the storm. I succeeded and was drifting with a tail wind when my motor conked."

"Motor conked?" interrupted Miss Valdmere. "What's that?"

"I beg your pardon. That's flying talk. It means that the engine stalled, refused to work. Well, anyway, I landed about twelve miles southeast of here, waited until the storm was over—and now I'm back."

"But where's your airplane? You came here in a car."

"It's standing near the trail, not far from the

place where we ran out of gasoline. I drove your car up here."

"You never told me you could fly," Miss Valdmere accused him.

"I can pilot an airplane much better than I can ride a broncho," he grinned. "I'm not a full-fledged pilot yet but I soon will be. Philo and I work for the same company in Minneapolis. I'm taking a course in flying, while Philo is learning the mechanical end. He's a ground man—a mechanic."

"I've always wanted to go up myself," Miss Valdmere told him.

Ted laughed. "You'll have your chance soon, Miss Peggy, provided Mrs. Strebbing doesn't object to staying alone. Let's go over and ask her."

Mrs. Strebbing proved to be a pleasant, motherly old person, for whom Ted immediately formed a strong liking. When the situation was explained to her, she laughed merrily.

"Afraid to stay alone," she cried. "Why should I be? I've lived in this region for nearly forty years. In that time I've been alone more than once and I've never seen anything to be afraid of." She turned to Miss Valdmere. "Of course, you must go, dear, if you really feel that it is the thing to do."

"You're certainly kind," said Ted, wringing her hand. "It is very important that Miss Valdmere should accompany me."

Not long afterward they bade good-bye to the brave little woman and made their way over to the waiting car. Miss Valdmere was tremendously excited. She chattered like a child and asked many questions. Was Ted sure they would find her father? Was he in good health? Had he been mistreated? How long did it take to fly over to the place where Ted had left Philo and Mr. Evanson?

As yet Ted had not told her of the man at Brownsville, posing as her father. He had said nothing about Evanson's story or of the photograph printed in the *Lancet*. This was no oversight on his part but the outcome of mature deliberation.

"If I tell her," he reasoned, "it may have a tendency to confuse her. When I take her to Brownsville, she'll know at once that that man is an imposter."

And in truth, this seemed highly probable. He and Philo and the public at large might be fooled by a clever deception, but it was almost certain that Miss Valdmere would instantly detect the impersonation. She and she alone could solve the perplexing problem.

Now that he had acquired the monoplane, Ted was certain that it would not take long to find the missing scientist. Already he had made his plans. Returning to the vicinity of the bandits' camp, flying low, he would keep a careful lookout for the

unfortunate professor.   During the three or four
hours that remained before the coming of darkness,
much could be accomplished.

Arriving at the place where he had left the monoplane, he spoke to Miss Valdmere.

"You won't be afraid to go up?" he asked.

"No, Ted," she replied.

"That's fine," he smiled.   "Now, Miss Peggy,
please listen to me carefully, because after we take
off there won't be much chance to talk.   It isn't fair
to keep you in ignorance of what I propose to do, so
I'll outline my plan briefly."

"All right, Ted, I'm listening."

"First of all, I'm going to fly to the Japs' camp
to find out for sure whether or not your father has
been recaptured.   If he isn't there, I'll try to find the
posse under Brent and Strebbing and then Philo and
Mr. Evanson.   If your father hasn't been located, I'll
keep right on going, flying low and searching everywhere until darkness sets in.   Then we'll return to
Brownsville and come out tomorrow morning to continue the search."

Miss Valdmere nodded her head to indicate that
she understood.

"How long will it take us to reach the Japs'
camp?" she asked.

"Not over half an hour," he told her.   "That's the
great advantage of an airplane and one reason why I

think we'll not be long in achieving our purpose."

"It's perfectly wonderful!" she clapped her hands. "Now is there any way in which I can help you?"

"Keep a sharp lookout incessantly," he instructed. "Use the telephone when you want to speak to me—and speak to me only when it's important. Remember you're my observer now. Piloting the plane, I won't have the opportunity to look about that you have. There's splendid visibility and I'm quite sure that nothing will escape your attention."

The girl's face grew very serious and she looked up at the youthful pilot, determination in her eyes.

"You may depend upon it, Ted, I'll do my very best."

"I'm sure of that, Miss Peggy," he smiled. "Now if you'll take your place in the rear cockpit, I'll tune up the motor. We'll be away in a few minutes."

Following the preliminary of warming up, Ted clambered aboard, placed his feet on the rudder bar, threw the stick forward and they taxied down the field. While they were zooming skyward, in an effort to reassure her, he turned his head and grinned back.

Thereafter, he was too busy piloting his craft to pay much attention to the fair young passenger sitting behind. Remembering his own first experience, he devoutly hoped that she would not be as frightened as he had been. For a girl, he thought, she displayed

remarkable courage. If their acquaintance should
ever ripen into a long and lasting friendship, it was
possible that she might learn to fly under his guid-
ance. Perhaps some day she might come to love this
form of adventure as much as he did himself. Where,
he wondered, could he find a more apt pupil than she.
A girl who could ride bronchos and——

His reflections were interupted by hearing the
buzzer ringing loudly. Leaning over, he put his ear
to the 'phone.

"See men below us," announced the voice of Miss
Valdmere, steady enough yet somehow hinting of the
excitement she felt. "Eight men in the party, Ted.
Thought you might want to know."

CHAPTER XXI.

AN IMPORTANT QUESTION

TED executed a right bank and came back. In order to determine with any degree of certainty who the eight men were, it would be necessary to make his way to a lower altitude. Dropping the nose of his machine, he planed down hundreds of feet until he was flying so low that he was barely missing the projecting tops of the hills. In flying parlance, he was hedge-hopping. He was so close to the earth now that he could easily make out who the men were. As they both had expected—the posse! He could pick out Brent's figure from among the rest and wished he could go down and talk to him.

Again the voice spoke in the 'phone:

"Father is not there. Do you intend to stop?"

"No," Ted called out his reply. "Nothing we can do here. We'll continue westward and try to locate the bandits' camp."

In spite of his belief that this would not be very difficult, he was compelled to circle for nearly an hour before he found it. The Japs were camped in a deep valley, a few miles west of the deserted cabin, from which he had set out that same afternoon. The discovery of the hostile camp threw them in a state of intense excitement which increased as they planed down to investigate.

Then, for the first time since he had undertaken to put his plan into operation, Ted wished that Miss Valdmere were not with him. There had been no danger in approaching close to the posse, but there was danger, and plenty of it, in swooping down upon the Japs. Ted literally held his breath as the big monoplane flew earthward on that first reconnoitering dive. Every moment he expected to hear a bullet whipping through the air. He was sure the Japs would anticipate their design and open fire. He waited breathlessly.

Lower and lower swooped the plane, Ted's heart racing in his breast like a runaway engine. He wondered why they didn't shoot. The suspense was awful. Whatever happened, he hoped no bullet would find its way to the rear cockpit, where Miss Valdmere sat. Presently they had darted straight over the huddled group below and were rising again to make another circle. While he was executing this manoeuver, he leaned forward and touched the buzzer.

"Hello—hello, Miss Peggy!" he called frantically in the 'phone.

"Yes, Ted, I hear you."

"Make out any of the party?"

"All Japanese so far as I can see. In order to make sure, you'd better go back again."

"Just what I'm planning, Miss Peggy. Watch carefully."

Three times in all they made that perilous downward swoop over the enemy's camp. And three times was enough, for it was apparent that Professor Valdmere was not there.

Afterward he and Miss Valdmere circled over the hills, endeavoring to find a trace of the missing scientist. The sun had slipped down below the horizon and already the hills were flinging out darkling shadows that made the search increasingly difficult. In a few more minutes, Ted perceived, they must abandon their work for the day and return to Brownsville. But he didn't like to do this until after he had had a talk with Philo and Mr. Evanson, who, he hoped, might have found the professor during the course of the afternoon.

The trouble was, he hadn't the slightest intimation of their whereabouts. While he had been manoeuvering through the hills neither he nor Miss Valdmere had seen them. Where were they? Could it be possible that his chum and Mr. Evanson had been succesful in their quest and had found the famous scientist?

Almost in despair, he finally came to the conclusion that Philo and Mr. Evanson had gone back to the cabin. Even though darkness was coming on, he and Miss Valdmere could slip over there and find out. He could make a landing on the plateau, just as Stugis had done, and afterward take off and wing his way over to Brownsville as he had originally planned.

Notifying Miss Valdmere of this change in his itinerary, he turned more to the north and, a few minutes later, just as dusk had begun to obscure the world, he banked for his descent and came down safely upon the same field from which he had made his departure nearly six hours before.

Owing to the fact that he had not been able to see very well, he had made his landing at the southern instead of the northern end of the plateau, nearly a quarter of a mile from the cabin. This, of course, necessitated a short journey through the dark. A few minutes after they had embarked upon this, Ted threw up his hands and gave a shout of joy.

Miss Valdmere stopped short.

"Goodness, Ted, how you startled me. What made vou do that?"

Glowing with happiness, Ted moved over toward her and pointed away through the dark.

"Look over there!" he instructed.

Miss Valdmere caught her breath.

"A light!" she cried excitedly. "So they're really here. You made a good guess, Ted."

"They're making a campfire, a sort of beacon to guide us. Philo probably heard our plane go over his head a little while ago and he hurried out to start a fire, thinking that it would help me in making the landing and at the same time show us that they were here."

"Do you suppose that they heard us when we came down at the southern side of the plateau?"

"Of course, they did. I'm willing to bet that both Philo and Mr. Evanson are on their way to meet us right now. I'll certainly be glad to see them. Maybe they have some news."

"Do you mean that they may have Father with them?" cried the girl.

Ted laughed. "I don't want to raise any false hopes after all the disappointments you've had, but it is possible. Gee whiz, here they are now. I can hear somebody up ahead. Hallo! Hallo!"

An answering shout re-echoed up ahead and soon afterward a muffled figure waded through the deep shadows toward them. An excited voice rang out:

"Is that you, Ted?"

"Right, old top. And Miss Valdmere too."

"Cracky!" Philo gave vent to his favorite ex-clamation.

"Don't keep us in suspense," Ted urged him. "Have you been successful? Why didn't Mr. Evanson come with you?"

"Because——" even in the deep obscurity Ted could see Philo throwing out his chest—"because, Ted, Miss Valdmere—well, I might as well confess that we have succeeded in our mission. Professor Valdmere is with us."

Although both had hoped that this might be the case, neither Miss Valdmere nor Ted were prepared for the startling revelation. The former uttered a queer, half-smothered little shriek and sat down right where she was and began to cry. Ted merely stood there, mouth gaping.

"Thank God for that. After all this trouble!" he finally managed to articulate. "Philo, tell us how it happened. Did you find him near the place where you and he were separated last night?"

"Nothing of the kind. We went over to the Jap's camp and got him."

"What's that!" Ted's eyes were popping. "You mean you——"

"I do mean it. A real encounter, if you please, with bullets flying and all that. The most thrilling experience I've ever had, and one I don't care to go

through again.   I won't take any credit because
it was Mr. Evanson who really bore the brunt of
the fighting.   Ted, I want to tell you he's superb.
Masterful!"

In his excitement, Philo was talking fast and at
this point he was compelled to pause for breath.

"I'm glad you were successful in making the
rescue," Ted contrived to crowd in the words.

Miss Valdmere rose to her feet.

"Please take me to him right away.   Philo—Ted
—please let's hurry.   I can't wait any longer.   I
must see Dad."

As they went forward, Philo recounted his experiences.   With true story-teller's zeal, he painted
a very vivid picture of the rescue of Professor
Valdmere.   With becoming modesty, he told his
two interested hearers how he had escorted the
famous scientist out of danger while Evanson had
held the Japs at bay.

"We took them completely by surprise," he informed them.   "Just as soon as we discovered the
professor was with them, we crept down through the
rocks and were right in their midst before we were
detected.   Mr. Evanson was a few feet ahead of
me.   He jumped to his feet, pointing his revolver
straight at them, calling out that he would shoot
down the first man who made a move.   They were
bunched together in a little group, holding some

sort of a conference and he really had the drop on them. At the same time he ordered me to hurry over and escort the professor to a place of safety.

The professor seemed a little dazed and at first I had difficulty in getting him to come with me. He must have gone through some terrible experiences, judging from the way he acted. I honestly do not believe, Miss Valdmere, that he recognized me at all. I was compelled to take him by the arm and literally drag him away from the Jap camp. Evanson covered our retreat, at the point of his revolver, afterward engaging them in a pitched battle, in which he very nearly lost his life."

They were near the northern end of the plateau now and Ted could see Mr. Evanson and Professor Valdmere awaiting their coming. They stood near the campfire which Philo had kindled, the former close to the flickering blaze, the latter within the reflection cast by the fire but at a point where the revealing light merged with the darkness.

It was the first time Ted had ever seen the renowned scientist in the flesh. Something closely akin to awe came over him. His eyes seemed to freeze upon the man and, in that one close all-encompassing scrutiny, he was sure that there could be no question whatsoever as to his identity. In that instant, all the doubt engendered by the story

Evanson had told, abruptly left. They had found the real Professor Valdmere at last.

An then, suddenly, a great thrill went through him. Miss Valdmere had given one swift, searching look at the man, then stumbled forward, a glad cry on her lips.

"Father!"

An eternity seemed to pass while the girl bounded across the space that separated them. Ted's heart leaped. His plan had worked. Here indeed, was positive proof that the waiting figure, limned there near the shadow, was the real Professor Valdmere and not the imposter.

And yet while he was thinking this and exulting in his heart over the fact that father and daughter were again reunited, he received a rude jolt that sent his hopes crashing to the ground.

When she had approached to within a few feet of the man, a strange thing happened. Miss Valdmere suddenly shrank back, as if she had received a blow in the face. The calm and serenity, which had heretofore distinguished the man, became erased. He, too, fell back a few paces, his face working queerily, and before anyone could stop him, had darted into the shadow and was gone.

The tense stillness that followed this remarkable action, was broken by Miss Valdmere herself who stumbled forward, then slid to the ground, where she broke into a violent paroxysm of weeping.

As for Ted, he stood riveted to the spot, stunned by the swiftness of events, wracking his mind in an effort to grasp the meaning of it all. In a sort of confused fashion he became aware of movement around him :—Evanson darted out into the darkness in hot pursuit of the man, Philo stooping down to comfort Miss Valdmere, and he himself standing opposite the fire, a revolver, which he could not remember having snatched from its holster, gripped tightly in his right hand.

In the next moment his chum had stumbled wearily to his feet, glaring at Ted as if he suspected that that young man had in some unaccountable manner been responsible for the unusual happening.

"I want you to tell me," he demanded from between set lips, "what in the name of reason and common sense got into that fool of a father of hers. Why did he run away?"

Ted was aghast.

"Do you mean to tell me you don't know?" he inquired savagely.

"Certainly I don't know."

"He didn't want to meet her, that's why. Good gracious, Philo, it's as plain as the nose on your face. That man is the imposter, the false Professor Valdmere."

"Good heavens! It can't be!"

"Why not?"

"But—but," trembled the other, "you heard her call out to him in that queer, choked voice. You heard her say Father, didn't you? Do you suppose for one moment that if that wasn't the real Professor Valdmere, her own flesh and blood, she'd have been taken in like that. Come, come, Ted, this thing has begun to work upon your mind. You're too suspicious."

"Suspicious, my foot! You don't need to take my word for it, you can ask her. She was fooled only for a minute. Then she saw her mistake and drew away from him as if he had been a reptile."

"No doubt, he's changed a lot. Why wouldn't he after all that has happened?"

"I tell you, her dad is the man back there at Brownsville."

CHAPTER XXII.

TED AND PHILO CONFER.

It was Miss Valdmere who finally dissipated any doubt Philo might have had by suddenly sitting up, daubing at her eyes and declaring in an injured voice:

"He's not my father. He's no more my father than you are and I hate him—hate him—hate him ——" Her voice broke and she covered her face with her hands.

"Keep quiet," Ted admonished his chum in a whisper, "or she'll become hysterical. Better not say any more about it. She's reached the limit of her endurance."

"What do you think we ought to do?" trembled Philo.

"Let's get out of her hearing where we can talk. There's something important I want to ask you."

Following a comforting word or two for Miss Valdmere, they withdrew to a more secluded spot, where Ted turned upon his chum eagerly.

"I want you to put on your thinking cap, Philo,

and help me out. I've spent hours in pondering over this case and I really believe I'm beginning to see a little light."

Philo merely grunted.

"Beginning to get an inkling of what it's all about," Ted hurried on.

Philo grunted again. "Pshaw, Ted, what's the use?" he inquired despondently. "You're only wasting your time. I tell you nothing will ever come of it. There's only one thing I'm sure of, and that is that this is a madman's plot—without rhyme or reason."

Ted reached over and touched his chum's arm.

"Philo," he inquired earnestly, "are you going to desert Miss Valdmere at this late hour? Are you a quitter? Do you propose to throw up your hands like a weakling and let things shape their own course? It isn't a bit like you, Philo."

The ruse worked. It was just as Ted had anticipated. The young man, slouching there despondently in the inky shadow of the rocks, suddenly gave a snort of anger and, reaching forward, seized Ted's wrists in a grip of steel.

"Don't you call me a quitter, by golly, or I'll wring your fool's neck. What are you trying to insinuate?"

"But you've just intimated that were were licked.

You said that I was wasting my time. I inferred, of course, that you were through and——"

Philo relaxed his iron hold of the other's wrists and stepped back, making an unintelligable noise in his throat.

"And I can't see how Miss Valdmere can get along if we give up the ship now," concluded Ted.

"I had no intention of giving up," roared Philo, touched to the quick. "You have me wrong, Ted —altogether wrong. I'll stick until the cows come home. I'll—I'll—nobody can say I'm a dirty quitter."

"Of course, not," the other pacified him. "I really don't blame you for being discouraged."

"I'm not discouraged!" flamed Philo. "Not a bit of it!"

"You really feel that we can match our wits against theirs?" Ted feigned astonishment.

"Why, certainly we can."

"And beat them at their own game?"

In one gulp Philo swallowed hook, line and sinker.

"Don't see why not."

"Well, I'm so glad you think so," Ted sighed with relief. "It's cheering to hear you say that. I had formed a number of impressions concerning this case and I might be able to arrive at some really astonishing conclusions if only there was someone who could give me a bit of advice."

"What is it you'd like to know?" asked his chum.

"I've been wondering if you held the same views I do concerning the real Professor Valdmere's enemies. Is there more than one faction, in conflict with each other, or are they all different groups of the same organization, all working under one leader?"

"I don't believe I quite understand you, Ted."

Ted hesitated a moment before answering.

"Here's what I mean, Philo: Are the Japs and Russians working together, or are they not?"

Philo did not hesitate. "My personal opinion is that they're two separate organizations," he responded.

Ted gave a little exclamation of satisfaction.

"That coincides with my belief. But here's a harder nut to crack: Are the Japs out here in the hills in any way connected with the group of men now holding the real Professor Valdmere on his estate at Brownsville?"

"Look here," protested Philo, "I think you're taking too much for granted. In the first place, how do you know the person at Brownsville is the real Professor Valdmere; and, in the second place, what leads you to believe that there is a group of men there holding him prisoner, as you have put it?"

"I know the person at Brownsville is the real Professor Valdmere," Ted replied, "because his own daughter has just proved it. I am almost equally confident that he is being held prisoner because there are a number of facts that point to such an inference."

"What are they?"

"If he had been his own free agent, he'd have given the demonstration, wouldn't he? Another thing, he'd have taken steps to apprehend the person or persons who rifled his safe. Still another point —and I think you'll be convinced—why hasn't something been done about Miss Valdmere. Why hasn't he tried to find her? She's his daughter, isn't she?"

"You bet she is," declared Philo, "There, at least is one person who's genuine."

"Very well, then, it must be apparent to you that Professor Valdmere is what I have said, virtually, if not in reality a prisoner on his estate at Brownsville."

"Ted, you're shrewd," complimented his chum. "I'm beginning to see it all myself. Yes, I'm prepared to admit now the existence of a third group of crooks."

"I'm glad I've won you over," laughed Ted.

"Now let's get back to our original problem: Are the Japs and the gang at Brownsville working together?"

For a time there was a deep silence. Ted could hear his chum shifting about uneasily and then presently draw a deep breath.

"I'm stuck," he acknowledged finally. "I'll have to admit I'm stuck. Say what a tangle everything is in. Perhaps if I wasn't so sleepy and tired and disgusted I might be able to figure it all out."

He drew another deep breath, changed his position once more, then:

"By golly, wait a minute! I'll take that all back. I have it now. They're the same gang."

Ted could scarcely conceal his elation. Bit by bit, his own findings were being verified. He stepped forward and patted the other's shoulder.

"Good boy, Philo! Tell me how you know."

"That note Miss Valdmere found in the office. It led her right into the hands of these Japs. Must have wanted to get her away from the estate for some reason. Anyway, it makes the connection between the two groups almost conclusive. But what about the Russians? Looking at this case from this new angle, one could almost believe that they, too, were members of the same organization."

"Except for one thing," Ted reminded him. "The Japs are shrewd, clever, ingenius, possessing a high grade of intelligence. And what's true of them is also true of the gang at Brownsville. But the Russians are a low, vulgar crowd, brave enough, perhaps, yet somehow not in a class with the others. It's hard to accept them in that connection."

"No doubt you are right. But listen, Ted, we'd better hurry back. Just now I thought I heard someone over there near the cabin."

"Probably Mr. Evanson returning," surmised Ted. "Wonder if he succeeded in capturing the imposter."

Hurrying over to the cabin, they found Mr. Evanson standing near Miss Valdmere and gazing moodily into the fire. He looked up as the boys approached.

"Gave me the slip," he declared with a trace of exasperation. "I was sure I'd overtaken him. Oh, well, perhaps I'll have better luck in the morning."

"I wouldn't waste any more time on him," advised Ted. "There is other and more important work to be done. I have been hoping that you and Philo would return to Brownsville tonight with Miss Valdmere and me. Guess I'll take off before it gets any later."

"Want to smash the plane?" asked Philo. "You're a fool if you try it."

"Why?"

"The plateau is rougher at its southern end. There

are plenty or rocks. You were lucky in landing, but
you might not be so lucky in taking off. You can't
afford to smash another man's machine. How'd
you ever replace it?"

"You're right, Philo. I'll wait until morning,"
Ted capitulated. "Just the same, it'll be very un-
comfortable here for Miss Valdmere. Not even a
bed to sleep in."

"Please don't mind me," said the girl, trying to
appear cheerful. "I'll manage somehow. I'm getting used to roughing it."

"You'll have pretty fair quarters after all," Philo
informed her. "You see, we thought that man was
your father and expected him to stay here tonight,
so Mr. Evanson and I fairly outdid ourselves in
providing a place for him. We've scrubbed out the
cabin and put clean grass in one of the bunks. I'll
admit it isn't a palace but you'll be quite comfortable, I think. I'm glad you're going to occupy that
cabin, Miss Valdmere, instead of that rascally imposter."

"Thank you very much, Philo," said the girl.

"If you had succeeded in catching him, Mr. Evanson," Philo went on, "nothing would please me
more than to tie him up by the heels and let him
dangle over the edge of the plateau until he had
occasion to repent of his sins."

Mr. Evanson laughed. "I think I'd have got

him easily if it hadn't been so dark. He timed his escape well."

"And a lot of good it'll do him," cut in Ted. "The ranchers' posse under Mr. Brent and Mr. Strebbing is on the way here and will be very apt to capture them all before tomorrow night."

"Hope so," grinned Philo. "Those cowboys know the country well, and, if they live up to their reputation, they know how to handle a gun."

"If you don't mind," said Miss Valdmere in a weary voice, "I think I'll retire."

"I'll show you over to your hotel," offered Philo. "Everything is all ready for you. Mr. Evanson and I found the stub of a candle this afternoon and it will light you. You can bolt the door on the inside and feel perfectly safe. We even put newspapers over the windows for curtains."

They had started to move away, when suddenly Miss Valdmere stopped short.

"Where do the rest of you intend to sleep?" she asked.

"Mr. Evanson and Philo will sleep in the cabin of the monoplane," answered Ted.

"But what about you?"

"I'm not sleeping at all tonight," he replied. "You see, Miss Valdmere, someone ought to guard the camp. Just a precaution, of course. Doubt if anyone will come to bother us."

Now, as it happened, neither Philo nor Mr. Evanson had heard of this arrangement. While Ted had been speaking, the two regarded him thoughtfully.

"When were you elected custodian of this camp?" inquired the young ground mechanic. "I must say, Ted, you take a lot of responsibility upon yourself."

"Not at all," smiled the other. "You and Mr. Evanson have had a hard day and certainly deserve a night's rest. You've walked miles today, while all I've done is to sit still and pilot an airplane. This sentry's job will give me a chance to stretch my legs."

"That doesn't seem fair," objected Mr. Evanson.

"Please don't look at it that way," laughed Ted. "I'm much fresher than either one of you. I'm used to going without sleep. I'm the logical candidite for the job and I won't feel happy if you fellows insist upon sharing it with me."

"Suit yourself," yawned Philo. "Don't try to dissuade him, Mr. Evanson. Won't do you a bit of good. When he gets like that he's more ornery and preverse than a whole army of obstinate elephants."

CHAPTER XXIII.

GROPING FOR CLUES.

DURING that long, lonely vigil Ted had plenty of leisure in which to ponder over the case. He felt that he could neither rest nor sleep until he had arrived at some satisfying explanation of all the strange events that had taken place since that morning, two days before, when he and Philo had first met Miss Valdmere. Pacing back and forth through the dark, piece by piece, he reviewed the intricate windings of the plot the conspirators had woven around the famous scientist. Though there were still a great many things he could not understand, he was confident now that at last he was on the right track to solving the mystery.

Miss Valdmere's repudiation of the person whom they had been following, and who, up until tonight they had been sure was the girl's father, had done much to simplify the case. Ted was certain now that the real Professor Valdmere was the man at Brownsville. He had probably been there all the time, held prisoner on his own esate. There seemed to be no other conclusion possible.

Accepting this very unusual state of affairs, however, had a tendency to enshroud still deeper in mystery certain other happenings. For example, how could one find a motive for the blood-stained note found in her father's office by Miss Valdmere? What was the meaning of the hare-and-hounds' chase up here to the hills? Why, above all, had the conspirators wasted so much valuable time and effort upon the girl?

These were the questions that perplexed Ted most of all. How inexplicable, how foolish, how unreasonable seemed to be the actions of the crooks. Judging from the care and trouble they had taken to lure the girl away from the estate, one might almost suppose that for some reason, yet to be discovered, the whole case centered around her. From the very beginning she had played into their hands. What had been their motive?

Strive as he would, he could find no reasonable solution. Like a huge wall, towering to a vast height, it seemed to confront him. It tantalized and maddened him. There seemed to be no way to get around it or over it. It defied him at every turn. He was almost on the point of giving up, when suddenly through his mind there flashed a vivid rememberance. In his blind groping for clues he seized upon it as a drowning man might seize upon a straw. It was something Philo had told him yesterday, shortly after they had been reunited. It was the message given to his chum by the imposter. He was sure that it must have some direct bearing upon the case. He could remember the words of the message as clearly as if he had heard them only a few minutes before:

"If you should escape and I don't, will you tell my daughter to go immediately to the bank at Brownsville, open her safety-deposit box, take home the papers I have entrusted to her care and read them carefully."

Over and over, Ted kept repeating that message, studying it word by word, sure at last that he had discovered the real key to the mystery.

"If you should escape and I don't," he mused. "By golly, I have it. The alleged professor did not escape that night, and for a very good reason. For two very good reasons. In the first place, he didn't want to escape because he wasn't the real Professor Valdmere, and, in the second place, all that business of escaping was merely a ruse, a carefully thought-out plan on the part of the crooks. They fully expected that Philo would go directly to Miss Valdmere and deliver that message. They wanted her to carry out those instructions: *'Open her safety-box, take home the papers I have entrusted to her care and read them carefully.'* "

Ted was thrilled. A new light flooded his mind.

Breaking off his ruminations, he started forward, dancing and shouting for joy.

"I have it! I have it!" he cried in a queer, wondering voice. "I can see it all now. Thank God, I have it!"

Under the pressure of his intense excitement, he whooped and shouted again. A great gladness was surging through him. He had begun to feel that his heart would burst with happiness engendered by his newly-discovered secret, when he heard the creak of a door and a voice, frightened and tremulous.

"O, Ted, is that you?"

"Miss Valdmere!" Called back to his senses, he stood stock-still, smitten with remorse. What a fool he'd been, yowling and prancing about in the middle of the night like a demented savage. But the damage had been wrought now. He made his way through the dark, calling to her:

"Please don't be frightened, Miss Peggy. Everything is all right. I'm sorry I awoke you. I forgot myself. But it's good news. Stand right there and I'll come to you."

When he joined her, she was trembling violently.

"What has happened?" she cried out.

"I think I have solved this case," Ted explained to her. "I'm so happy. I'm sure now that I can release your father and bring all his enemies to justice."

Where is my father?" she demanded.

"At Brownsville."

"How did he get there?"

"He's been there all the time," he answered. "But, Miss Peggy, you won't mind if I don't tell you everything right now. I want to ask you a few questions. They are very important and you must answer them if you can. If we're to release your father, we must move carefully, make no mistakes. Otherwise something terrible may happen to him. You must trust me implicitly."

"I do, Ted—I do. I'll answer your questions, of course. What are they?"

"First of all," Ted could scarcely repress the eagerness in his voice, "why didn't you tell me that your father had entrusted his secret to you?"

"What secret?" she gasped.

"The secret of the Atomic Ray."

"But, Ted," she cried out in bewilderment. "What makes you think that he has? Why—why, I don't understand you. He never took me in his confidence about any of his business affairs and I can't remember that he ever entrusted me with any secret."

For a moment Ted was nonplussed. He gave a little groan of disappointment.

"Think, think, Miss Peggy," he begged. "You

must be mistaken. What about your safety-deposit box at the Brownsville bank? Didn't your father give you some papers to put in it?"

An eternity seemed to pass before Miss Valdmere answered, and not until then did the terrific strain upon Ted relax.

"Why, of course," she exclaimed gleefully. "How stupid I am. But you're mistaken, Ted, about the secret. They were just some old papers belonging to father—I'm sure they couldn't be important—which he asked me to keep with my things."

"And you put them in the bank?" he asked breathlessly.

"Yes, that's exactly what I did. I had forgotten all about it."

"Did you examine any of those papers, Miss Peggy?"

"Why, no, of course, I didn't."

"And at the time—please think back, Miss Peggy, and help me all you can—wasn't your father worried?"

"I didn't notice particularly," she answered. "Perhaps he was. The papers he handed me were in a bulky parcel—quite heavy. He gave them to me on the afternoon of the day I returned home from school in New York."

"Did your father accompany you when you took the papers to the bank?"

"No, he sent Mr. Bernard with me. It seemed foolish at the time, but he insisted upon it. Mr. Bernard is Dad's private secretary, as you probably know. I never liked him because he—he tried to make love to me one time long ago and—and— well, you know how it is—I dreaded to have him near me."

"Did Mr. Bernard ask you about the papers while you were driving to the bank?"

"No," replied the girl. "As a matter of fact, Mr. Bernard drove the car and I held the package in my arms. When we reached the bank, I told Mr. Bernard to wait for me and I went right in, rented a safety-deposit box and put the package, together with a few trinkets of my own, in it."

"Now, Miss Peggy, I want to ask you one or two more questions and then I'll be through. Everything is working out just as I thought it would. The mystery is a mystery no longer. Tomorrow, Miss Peggy—you may rely upon it—you'll be reunited with your father."

A deep silence followed this declaration. In the darkness, Miss Valdmere reached out and touched the young man's arm.

"I sincerely hope so, Ted, although it seems almost too good to be true. Please go on with your questions."

"Is there a combination for your safety-deposit box or has it a key?"

"A key," she answered.

"Have you the key with you?"

"Yes, here in my purse."

Ted felt little tremors of fear and apprehension running up and down his spine.

"That's just what I was afraid of," he endeavored to keep his voice steady. "Miss Valdmere—Peggy, we must wake Mr. Evanson and Philo and get away from here as quickly as we can."

CHAPTER XXIV

FLIGHT.

TED took Miss Valdmere by the arm, beseeching her to hurry. He realized now the danger they were in, realized for the first time how important it was to quit the plateau before the imposter returned with the Japs to seize the daughter of the famous scientist and secure the key that unlocked the box in the bank at Brownsville.

Arms linked together, they started foward on the dead run, scrambling and stumbling over the rocks.

"The Japs!" he panted. "The Japs! O, Miss Peggy, I'm terribly afraid they'll arrive before we can get safely away. Heaven help us if they come now. I——"

His voice died in his throat. To his inutterable horror and dismay, he perceived that they were already too late. Less than fifty yards ahead, there had suddenly arisen two shadowy forms to bar their way. Clutching at Ted in terror, Miss Valdmere emitted a piercing scream.

For a time Ted's blood seemed to congeal in his

veins. Wide-eyed with panic, he took two paces back, striving to regain control of himself, desperately trying to strangle the fear that rose up within him. All the while Miss Valdmere clung to him in terror.

Then calmness and decision came. With a quick motion, he thrust the girl almost roughly aside and clawed for his gun. The first to open fire, his bullet glanced off the rock, near which the nearest Jap was standing, striking a huge boulder thirty yards beyond. Immediately the figures of both men dropped out of sight but Ted did not pause. Twice more he fired in the general direction of his two hidden enemies, at the same time guiding Miss Valdmere past the Jap's barricade and heading toward the southern end of the plateau.

"Now," he instructed between set teeth, "your chance! Run! Toward the monoplane. I'll go slower and try to prevent them from following us."

Motioning to her frantically, he turned, looking back, his revolver sweeping the barricades of rocks, then he, too, followed quickly in her footsteps, continuing to fire at random. Presently he had used his last cartridge and was compelled to pause to reload. A bullet squashed in the ground at his feet. Gravel sprayed up in his face. He fired again. Perceiving a large rock close to one side of him, he jumped behind it, steadied his shaking arm on its smooth top, and fired thrice in rapid succession straight at the spot where he had seen the crimson flash of the Jap's gun.

After that, a venomous hissing in the air all about him, as the leaden messengers continued to fly, he turned and bolted in the direction Miss Valdmere had gone. So swiftly did he race along the plateau that, a few hundred yards farther on, he overtook her and together they flew along in their final spurt to the plane.

Almost there, they heard someone directly ahead shouting to them. Ted thrilled as he recognized Evanson's voice. Panting, struggling, they had just reached him when the silence was broken by a reverberating roar.

"I told Philo to start the motor," Evanson shrieked. "What's wrong? Are the Japs following you?"

Ted tried to answer but his breath caught in his throat, making speech impossible. He swayed there on his feet, possessing barely strength enough to take a few more steps. Despite the coolness of the night, the plateau seemed like a burning desert. Perspiration ran into his eyes. He was glad when Evanson, perceiving his plight, jumped forward to relieve him of the extra burden of assisting Miss Valdmere the remaining twenty feet over to the plane.

After that things happened with surprising swiftness. Philo had helped him into the front cockpit and had clambered in beside him, when a fiendish, unearthly yell echoed along the slope leading up to the top of the plateau. Surmising that the Japs were gathering to make an attack, Ted leaned forward and put the plane in motion. At that instant his chum called out lustily:

"Stop, Ted. Stop! We're safe now. Don't take off. Wait! The posse!"

Ted shut off the motor and the big monoplane taxied to a jarring stop.

"The posse!" he gasped. "Are you sure, Philo?"

"Certainly I'm sure," gleefully shouted the other. "I saw the horses just after we heard that outlandish shriek. Not Japs at all—cowboys! Pile out."

In the darkness outside they were soon surrounded by prancing horses and shouting men. One could hear the creaking of saddles, as riders dismounted. Gravel crunched under impatient feet. Finally, Ted recognized the familiar form of the sheepherder.

"Mr. Brent! Mr. Brent!" he shouted.

Leading his horse, the big man hurried over.

"We heard some shootin'. What trouble are you in now, Ted?"—laughing.

"Mr. Brent, the Japs attacked us a few minutes ago. They were starting to come up on this plateau but I think that your approach has frightened them away."

"We'll be ready for them if they come again," said the sheepherder. "Well, my boy, how are things going?"

"Pretty fair now, Mr. Brent," Ted replied. "I'll have to admit, though, that you came in the nick of time. How did you find out that we were here?"

"Early in the evenin' you had a fire burnin' an' we sort o' figgered it was your signal. Anyway, that's what brought us. A light up here on the plateau can be seen for miles. Mighty good thing you started it."

At this juncture, another horseman advanced toward them on foot. Perceiving him, the sheepherder called out:

"Strebbing, this boy tells me them pesky bandits is in this vicinity right now. What you reckon we'd better do, wait here or go after 'em?"

"Wait here," Strebbing answered promptly. "It's a little dark to do much chasing around. Better wait here an' see if they won't attack."

"That's what I think," Brent told him. "We can start out after 'em soon as the light comes. Ought to be daybreak in another two hours. By the way, Strebbing, who's lookin' after them prisoners?"

"Danny Merril's watchin' 'em now."

"Prisoners!" Ted's eyes opened wide. "Did you succeed in capturing a few of the Japs before you arrived here, Mr. Brent?"

"No," the sheepherder spoke disgustedly. "Your friends, them pesky Russians."

Ted laughed. "So you bumped into them, too?"

"No trouble pickin' them up," Brent declared modestly. "Wouldn't have bothered with 'em at all only we sort o' figgered the sheriff might want 'em before this business is cleared up. An' that reminds me, young feller, I got a message for you. Can you guess who it's from?"

"No," Ted stared incredulously.

"From a girl," laughed the sheepherder. "Mebbe you can savy now. Strebbing's mother is looking after her back there on my own range. She'll be mighty glad to know how everything is turnin' out."

"What did she say?" asked Ted, his eyes twinkling.

"It wasn't much, only to wish you good luck an' the hope that when you got back you'd bring her father with you. There's a mighty fine girl, young feller. Got lots of grit an' is as smart as you make 'em."

"Miss Valdmere is here," Ted launched his verbal bomb.

"What!" exploded Brent.

"Yes," answered Ted, laughing, "I picked her up this afternoon and brought her here in that same monoplane that flew down so close to you."

"Well, I'll be jiggered! Young man, you certainly can move fast. So that was you?"

"Miss Valdmere and I. We'd have stopped if there had been any place to land and if we hadn't been in such a hurry to get over this way and search for Professor Valdmere."

"What are you plannin' on doin' with that airship now?" asked Brent.

"We're taking off for Brownsville at daybreak," Ted replied. Miss Valdmere's father is there. We must get to him as soon as we possibly can."

Apparently this was too much for the groping Mr. Brent. For a full minute he stared at Ted, his mouth gaping open.

"One of us is loco for sure," he growled. "Did I hear you say her dad was in Brownsville?"

"Yes, Mr. Brent."

"How come? He must move a hull lot faster even than you do. How did he get over there so quick?"

Ted was too tired to enter upon a full and complete explanation of all that had taken place in the past few hours. He reached over, patting the hand of the kindly-hearted sheepherder.

"I'll be glad to give you all the particulars later on. For the present all I can say is that the man we thought was Professor Valdmere, and whom we have been following for so long, is a rank imposter. He's one of the crooks."

"Well, I'll be jiggered!"

"It's true, Mr. Brent."

"Well, I'll be jiggered!" exclaimed the sheep-herder for the third and last time.

CHAPTER XXV.

BROWNSVILLE ONCE MORE.

EARLY on the morning of Wednesday, June 26th, a large cabin monoplane, carrying a pilot and three passengers, sailed down out of a clear, sun-drenched sky and taxied to a stop in a field adjacent to Brownsville.

Clambering out of the cockpit, the young pilot consulted his watch, made his way over to the little group, one of whom was a young lady, and remarked in a cheerful voice:

"Just six o'clock. We have plenty of time to make all our arrangements." He paused and turned upon one of his passengers, a man of about middle age. "It is understood then, Mr. Evanson, that you are to proceed immediately to the sheriff's office?"

"Yes," nodded the man.

"And Miss Valdmere, Philo and I will make our way over to the business section of the town," the young pilot continued.

Again Mr. Evanson nodded.

"There ought not to be any chance for a mis-understanding," reflected Ted. "You have your work to do and we have ours. We are not to meet again, under any circumstances, until this thing is definitely settled. Do you think you'll be able to go through with it, Miss Valdmere?"

"I'm a little frightened, of course, Ted, but I am confident that I shall not fail. That would be ter-rible."

"I'm sure you'll not fail," Ted said confidently. "It won't be a pleasant experience, however. Never-theless, we know you'll come through with flying colors."

"Do you really believe the conspirators will recog-nize me?" she asked.

"Yes, I do," answered Ted. "You won't be in Brownsville ten minutes before they'll be aware of it. No doubt they have emmisaries everywhere. They'll watch you closely but I don't think they'll approach you or attempt to interfere with you in any way until they have determined what has brought you back to Brownsville. What we hope is that they'll come to the conclusion that you have really fallen into their trap and have come here to carry out the instructions contained in that mes-sage."

"Let us hope so, anyway," put in Mr. Evanson.

"What do you think they'll do when I enter the

bank?" asked Miss Valdmere, striving to keep her voice calm.

"A number of them will assemble outside," Ted told her, "that is, we assume they will. When you come out, they'll make a concerted rush toward you and seize the papers. Remember it isn't you they want but those papers. Do not be afraid. Do not falter, Miss Peggy. Even your father's safety may depend upon how you carry this thing out. But whatever you do, please don't risk bringing out the real papers containing the secret of the Atomic Ray."

"Let me get this thing straight," Philo suddenly cut in. "Do I infer that the formulae for the Atomic Ray are in Miss Valdmere's safety-deposit box?"

"That is what we believe," came the quick rejoinder. "In fact, we're almost sure of it."

"And you propose to send Miss Valdmere into the bank to get a false set of papers. You hope to fool the conspirators. Is that correct?"

"Yes, that's correct."

"I don't want to pick flaws in your plan," said Philo, "but I'm afraid it won't work. The crooks will examine the papers right away and discover they're false. You'll use a lot of blank sheets, I suppose, wrapped up in a package?"

Mr. Evanson placed a hand upon the young man's shoulder and shook him playfully.

"Come, come, my boy, I'm beginning to have a suspicion that you were asleep this morning when we made our plans. Ted's suggestion is to draw up these false papers in such a way as to make it appear that they are in code. I'm to do it this morning at the sheriff's office. There'll be just time enough to do this before the bank opens. Then I'll take them to the bank myself and give them to the cashier. The crooks do not know me so will suspect nothing. Further than that, I must not be seen with either of you boys or Miss Valdmere. We separate here."

Philo flushed with embarrassment. "Well, a fellow can't keep awake all the time. I did doze off, I'll admit. Now please tell me one more thing: When Miss Valdmere comes out of the bank with the false papers and the crooks overpower her and seize them, will a sheriff's posse be there to capture the crooks?"

"No," replied Ted. "That is what we planned at first but we rejected it for two reasons. The first one was that the crooks might become suspicious if a crowd of men, not of their party, gathered near the bank; and, in the second place we feel that such a course might endanger the life of Professor Valdmere."

"But Professor Valdmere is on his estate. How could it endanger his life?"

"They might kill him out of pure spite. Failing to secure the secret, their first thought, naturally, would be revenge. It would be much better to lead them to believe that they had really secured the secret. It is the thing they want, have been striving for since the beginning. As soon as they get possession of what they believe to be the real papers they'll depart—and depart hurriedly. Before this happens, however, picked men under the sheriff will form a cordon, guarding all the roads leading out of the village. So you can see the crooks will fly right into the net."

"It's an ambitious plan," remarked Philo. "Only one thing I don't like about it. It places Miss Valdmere in a very trying position."

The girl smiled at the perturbed young man.

"I'm willing to go through with it," she declared valiantly. "It is my duty to my father. I'm sure I'll carry it out successfully."

"When do you think you'll have those false papers ready," Ted turned to Mr. Evanson.

"By the time the bank opens," he answered. "However, to be on the safe side, it might be advisable for Miss Valdmere to delay entering the bank until about ten o'clock."

"Very well, then, we must separate.   Good-bye. Mr. Evanson."

"Good-bye and good luck to all of you," he responded, offering his hand.

Then, all of them strangely quiet, watched him make his way hurriedly across the field in the direction of the village.

CHAPTER XXVI.

PLANS MISCARRY.

At twenty minutes past eight, Philo, Ted and
Miss Valdmere were seated in the dining room of
the Grand Majestic Hotel eating a belated breakfast. They had chosen a table at the back of the
room for very obvious reasons, chief of which was
their somewhat unkempt appearance. Since entering they had made no attempt at conversation.
Covertly they were regarding the other guests and,
with the exception of Philo, whose appetite seemed
unimpared, they had little appetite for the food set
before them.

Miss Valdmere's face was very grave and
thoughtful. Watching her, Ted wondered if she
wasn't dreading the coming ordeal and was fearful
of what might happen. For his own part, he would
be more than glad when it was all over. There was
a strain upon him now which was rapidly sapping
his energy. Sleeplesness had made his eyes heavy
and his mind dull. His nerves were raw, constantly
on edge, and, for the life of him, he could not dis-
pel a queer obsession of some near menace.

In an effort to overcome this feeling, he tried to keep his thoughts turned in more wholesome channels. Indeed, why shouldn't he be happy? In a few more hours victory would be theirs. Miss Valdmere would pass the crucial test, the secret of the Atomic Ray would remain in the bank, the famous scientist would be reunited with his daughter —and all of the crooks would be captured. With this pleasing prospect almost within view how, he demanded of himself, could he be so foolish as to find room in his mind for doubt.

Nevertheless, the feeling persisted, not only persisted but grew to such formidable proportions that presently it had obliterated even that bright vision of appproaching victory. Noticing his deep absorption, Miss Valdmere spoke to him:

"What's the matter, Ted? Why don't you eat?"

"I can't. I'm too nervous. Wish we hadn't come in here."

Miss Valdmere smiled brightly.

"So that's what's worrying you. Well, you might as well dismiss it altogether. Nothing will happen. Everything will come out just as we have planned."

Philo looked up sharply. "See here, Ted, I'd like to know what's up. A while ago you were all enthusiasm. Now you're down in the dumps. You look more miserable and unhappy than any other person in this room."

Ted forced a smile. "I guess the reaction has set in now that we have reached the end of the road. Those crooks——"

"Ssh!" whispered his chum. "Not so loud! We'd better not talk too much. I have no wish to alarm either one of you but those two fellows sitting by that table—the second from the end, outside row—have been casting some rather curious glances our way. Perhaps they are members of the gang and have recognized us."

"I hope so," said Ted.

"Why do you hope so?" scowled Philo.

"I'll answer that question by asking you one: If Miss Valdmere isn't recognized, how can we carry out our plan?"

"Never thought of that,"—and Philo returned to the business of eating.

"How are we going to spend the time between now and ten o'clock?" Miss Valdmere inquired.

"That has been worrying me, too," Ted confessed. "I suppose though, that we'd better loiter around the business section of the town until the bank opens. In that way, the conspirators will be given every opportunity to see you. Then, too, Philo and I ought to make it a point to address you by your full name as often as possible."

He turned to his chum.

"Please remember that, Philo. From now on it's

Miss Valdmere this and Miss Valdmere that—as often as you can crowd in the word without appearing to be doing it for effect."

Philo pushed back his plate.

"I'll remember," he grinned. "And now that I have finished our breakfast—it was ever so good—what do you say to turn about the town?"

They had actually started away from the table when Ted held up his hand.

"Wait! I've just thought of something," he cried. "I know now," he lowered his voice and dropped back into his chair, "I know now just what to do, Miss Valdmere, so that the conspirators won't overlook the fact that you're in town. Why not pop into the telephone booth in the lobby just outside and call up Mr. Bernard, your father's private secretary. Tell him that you've just returned after an unsuccessful search for your father. Say that you've just had your breakfast at the Grand Majestic Hotel and that, following instructions contained in a message which you received from your father just before he ultimately disappeared, you are going over to the bank at ten o'clock to secure certain papers."

Miss Valdmere's eyes shone with admiration.

"What a capital idea, Ted. How did you happen to think of it?"

For some reason, however, Philo did not seem to share the enthusiasm of his two companions. He

sat, one hand firmly gripping the edge of the table,
his brow wrinkled in thought. Suddenly he leaned
forward, plucking at Ted's sleeve.

"Not quite so much speed, old timer. First, let's
think this thing out. If Miss Valdmere does as
you've just suggested, it will mean a complete re-
arrangement of our plans. In all probability this
private secretary—Mr. Bernard, I think you called
him—will slip down here in a car, meet you just
outside the bank and take you home."

"What if he does?" asked Miss Valdmere. "At
least, I'll see my dad."

"Don't be too sure about that," Philo told her.
"Perhaps you won't see him at all. The minute they
get you on the estate, they'll take away those false
papers, tie you up and throw you in a room somewhere. You wouldn't want that to happen, would
you?"

Ted's arm swept out in an impatient gesture.

"For goodness sake, Philo, don't talk so loud. It
won't do to sit here discussing this thing so openly.
Now that you have called my attention to it, I can
see for myself that there are a number of weak spots
in my suggestion to call up Bernard."

"It seems to me," said Miss Valdmere, "that it's
a good plan."

"No, on second thought, I'm sure Philo is right.

Whatever happens, you must not let them take you home."

"They may do that anyway," she objected. "I mean, even if I don't call up Mr. Bernard. How can we tell what may happen?"

Ted rubbed his forehead in despair.

"Anything is possible, of course. We have no way of ascertaining in advance just what they will do. Instead of snatching the papers away from you, they may——"

"Pshaw!" interrupted Philo. "We'll all be gray-headed if we keep on like this. Take my advice and don't tamper with your original plan."

"But there is always a chance that we may improve upon our original plan," Ted pointed out.

"Exactly what I think," agreed Miss Valdmere. "It may be a wise precaution to telephone Mr. Bernard. If there was only some good reason to give him for——"

Miss Valdmere never finished the sentence. Clear, low, deadly, a voice rang out behind them. At the same time, they heard the cushioned tread of advancing feet.

"You people may not be aware of it, but there are six men in this room, all heavily armed—and each one has you covered. Sit perfectly still and not a cry out of you! Keep your hands on top of the table!"

Phil and Ted twisted in their seats, goggling up into the unfriendly face. A man they had never seen before! Eyes hard as steel! One could see at a glance that here was a person that it wouldn't be the part of wisdom to oppose. His unyielding gaze swept the table.

"Thank you, that looks better. Miss Valdmere. if I were you, I wouldn't scream. It might annoy the other guests and besides a bullet fired from a gun at close range always makes a person look so messy. You wouldn't want that to happen, would you?"

An unoccupied chair stood near the table. Still glowering at them, he drew it toward him and sat down.

CHAPTER XXVII.

AN ULTIMATUM.

THE stranger hitched his chair forward, put his elbows on the table and stared straight into the eyes of the frightened girl.

"We won't waste any time," he announced in his smooth, oily voice. "Let's get right down to brass tacks, Miss Valdmere. You're powerless and must do exactly what I tell you."

"What do you want?" she trembled.

The man smiled—and it was a horrible smile. His dark eyes drilled into hers relentlessly.

"I'm giving you your choice, young lady, and it is your privilege to refuse or accede to our demands. By acceding them, no harm shall come to your father. If you refuse, he dies. That's plain, isn't it?"

He paused momentarily to let his meaning sink in.

"Now let me acquaint you with the situation. Please follow me in every detail. Professor Valdmere, your own flesh and blood, is in our hands. He has perfected a wonderful invention which he

has called the Atomic Ray. But instead of giving
this great discovery to the world, making it a boon
to all mankind, he proposes instead to use this potent
new force to advance his own mercenary interest
and the interests of a few powerful manufacturing
concerns, who will profit at the expense of the down-
trodden masses."

At that moment Miss Valdmere showed that she
was truly her father's daughter. Her face flamed
angrily.

"I don't believe it. It's a lie. Father intended
to give this discovery to the world. It is his life
work. He had hoped it might be a monument to
his memory."

The man's face twisted in a sardonic leer. He
made a gesture of disdain.

"We won't argue the matter. However, I know
I am right because we have offered Professor Valdmere a vast sum of money for his invention. He
refused us. So we have adopted the only logical
course open to us. We are taking the secret of the
Atomic Ray by force."

"Stealing it, you mean," Miss Valdmere's voice
was edged with contempt.

The stranger bowed mockingly.

"If it pleases you—yes! I'll not split hairs. What
I want to point out is that your father is a prisoner,
has been for two days. We had expected to find the

secret for the Atomic Ray in the steel safe in Professor Valdmere's office. It was not there. We tried to force your father to tell us. He is very stubborn and told us that he would much rather die. We really would have killed him on the afternoon of that first day had not Mr. Bernard, who has kindly consented to join us, deduced where the papers and formulas were. They are in the Brownsville bank in a safety-deposit box which you rented on the afternoon of Saturday, June 22nd."

"You seem to know all about it," sneered Miss Valdmere.

The man laughed coarsely. "Yes, we know more than you think we do. Our organization is very powerful. We know, for example, that you were in the hills, west of Langdon Prairie, only last night. We know the names of your friends here, Mr. Winters and Mr. Birch. We know that you flew to Brownsville early this morning in an airplane. All of you have been under close surveillance since your arrival."

"You haven't stated yet what you want Miss Valdmere to do," Ted reminded him.

The pupils of the man's eyes glinted like two steel points.

"I'm coming to that, don't worry. I shall be very specific in stating our demands. Briefly, Miss Valdmere has the choice of going to the bank and getting those papars for us, or not going to the bank and being a witness to the murder of her father— deliberately and in cold blood."

The implication was so horrible that all three of the young people started and turned deathly pale.

"On the other hand," the man went on, "if Miss Valdmere does accede to our demands, we will take her immediately to her father. We will harm no one."

"It's very kind of you," sputtered Ted.

"Your father will be waiting for you," hinted the man, wholly ignoring Ted's remark. "You can save your father's life by doing what we ask."

The silence that followed was exceedingly painful for all of them. Miss Valdmere lowered her gaze and sat staring at her plate, lips trembling and fingers working nervously with a button on the front of her blouse. It was a trying moment. Ted himself experienced a choking sensation as if ghostly, unseen fingers had encircled his neck and were slowly strangling the breath out of him. There could be no doubt as to what Miss Valdmere would decide. She was helpless. He sat staring at her as if fascinated. He saw her lips move, forming the words,

"I—I'll do it."

And then, while a look of triumph overspread the conspirator's face and he emitted an exclamation of approval, Ted saw the stricken girl lean forward over the table and bury her head in her arms.

It was an unusual tableau: Philo half leaning over the table, his face ghastly, the girl shivering in her chair, dry-eyed with horror, while only a few feet away, wholly oblivious of what was going on, people chatted gaily and waiters darted here and there through the crowded room.

Right across from where he sat, a large clock, hanging on the wall, told him the time. Four minutes to nine! In four more minutes the bank would be open. In four more minutes Miss Valdmere would be forced to cross the street and enter the bank for the ill-fated papers.

Ted's heart pumped furiously. If Miss Valdmere entered the bank promptly at nine, he was sure that the cause would be lost. He doubted very much whether Evanson would be in time. And even if he was, would not the conspirators, who seemed to know everything, frustrate him in the attempt to enter the bank. Surely if he and Philo were known to the conspirators, so would Evanson be as well. They had all come to Brownsville together. Perhaps agents of the gang had even followed Evanson to the sheriff's office.

Dejected, hopeless, he slumped back in his chair, eyes glued upon the clock across the room. If only there might be some way he could delay the proceedings. If only he might communicate with Miss Valdmere. If only the man would get up and cross over to one of the tables or even turn his head so that he might whisper one word of advice and comfort to the sorrowing girl. The big hand of the clock moved forward another space while the room seemed to reel about him.

Three minutes to nine!

Ted was desperate. How quickly the seconds slipped by.

Two minutes to nine!

Their captor pushed back his chair, put two fingers in the pocket of his vest and brought out his watch. He scowled as he glanced at it.

"Almost time for the bank to open, I believe," he remarked in a low tone.

Ted grasped at the proverbial straw in this time of dire need.

"I believe the bank opens at ten," he hazarded.

The man scowled again, still holding his watch.

"No, not these country banks. Nine o'clock. Are you ready, Miss Valdmere?"

The girl raised her drooping head, her face pallid with anguish. Ted felt a great surge of pity for her and anger, ill-concealed rage for the man.

"Miss Valdmere is in no position to go over there now," he pointed out. "After the shock she's just had," he glared across at their captor, "I think it is only fair that you give her a few minutes to herself, a chance to recover a little. Have you no gentlemanly instincts at all?"

Up until this time the conspirator had been deliberate, cold, domineering, but not until now had he shown a trace of anger. A red flush mounted to his forehead. He turned, snarling upon Ted.

"You keep out of this—understand?"

"I won't keep out of it," Ted flared back, in that moment deciding to throw all caution to the winds. "If you aren't enough of a gentleman to grant the slight request I'm asking for the sake of this poor girl, I'll—I'll do something myself."

"You! You!" The man's face was livid now. "What can you do?"

Ted did not falter. "I'll tell you what I can do. I can make a break for that door. Your gunmen will. be compelled to fire. It will make a rather awkward position for you, won't it? You may get me but I don't care. There is no earthly reason why you can't give this young lady, who is shocked and ill, a slight chance to recover. You've issued your ultimatum to Miss Valdmere. Now let me issue mine. Either you'll comply with my request or I'll run straight for the door. Suit yourself."

With a few bricks at his disposal, Ted had builded even better than he new. He was aware of this the next instant when the conspirator, seething with fury, nodded his acceptance of the terms laid down.

"All right, you young devil, have your own way. But no tricks, mind you, or I'll settle with you my-self. Miss Valdmere shall not leave my sight for one minute. Please get that clearly—not one minute—nor you either."

"That's your privilege," replied Ted.

"Very well," said the conspirator. "Lead the way to the lobby. We'll find a chair for Miss Vald-mere."

CHAPTER XXVIII.

TED GIVES BATTLE.

THE short respite given to Miss Valdmere passed with miraculous swiftness. It seemed to Ted as if they had barely settled back in their seats, when their captor, watch in hand, announced that it was fifteen minutes after nine.

"Time's up," he grunted. "You've had your little rest, young lady, so action is the password now. I'll accompany you to the bank and wait for you just outside. As for your friends," he turned glaring upon Ted, "they'll have to stay right here."

Ted was wondering how the conspirator could watch both Miss Valdmere and themselves, when a middle-aged man, clad in a gray suit, in response to some unseen signal detached himself from a small group standing a few feet away and strode quickly over. The conspirator nodded to him.

"Ed, you look after these two young men," he instructed in a low voice. "Don't move out of this lobby. Wait for me here. I'll be back in a few minutes."

With this.parting command, he swung on his heel
and he and Miss Valdmere walked toward the door.
Just as she was descending to the street, the girl
turned and her eyes met Ted's squarely. A peculiar
light seemed to burn there. It was as if she were
trying to speak with her eyes, to impart a message.

Ted smiled back at her, gulping down a lump in
his throat. What was she trying to tell him? Was
she thanking him because he had interceded in her
behalf? Was she saying goodbye? Did some terrible intuition tell her that they would never meet
again?

But whatever might be the meaning of that look,
he was confident that she understood clearly his
real reason for obtaining the fifteen minutes respite.
She must know that delay meant everything. He
was sure, too, that if the chance offered, she would
endeavor to resort to some subterfuge in order to
give Mr. Evanson more time.

Miss Valdmere and her grim escort made their
way through the crowd in the street below. They
had headed toward the bank, moving slowly. The
surging throng momentarily hid them from view.
When they reappeared, they were advancing across
the street still more slowly, the girl limping. Ted
guessed what that meant. In an effort at further
delay, she had pretended to sprain her ankle. He
observed that the man's arm was supporting her.

What became of them after that Ted never knew. Just then he heard the gruff voice of the man at his elbow, ordering him and Philo to the back of the room. One last look toward the street, and he was forced reluctantly ahead of his new guard to a more secluded corner, where a small group of men awaited them.

"Keep quiet, y'understand, an' no funny work," admonished the guard in a brutal, threatening voice. "There's a little matter we wanta attend right now."

What this matter was, soon became evident. The group suddenly pushed in around them laughing and slapping each other on the backs. They jostled and pushed each other playfully. Ted was at a loss to understand the meaning of this until he felt an encircling arm around his waist and the pressure of a hand against his hip. Then the human screen drew aside, but not before two revolvers were whipped out of sight—two revolvers that had formerly belonged to himself and Philo.

"Now, stand right where you are," the low, threatening voice continued.

Through it all Ted had been impressed with the ease and swiftness with which the crooks had worked. Under the eyes of at least a score of persons, guests of the hotel, they had carried out their manoeuver without attracting the slightest suspicion. It boded ill for the hope that any plan that his poor mind might devise could circumvent them. It emphasized again the power and cunning of the organization. How could Mr. Evanson, Miss Valdmere's kind ally, upon whom so much depended, escape the meshes of the net the conspirators had spread?

Then, and not until then, Ted gave up hope. He, Philo and Miss Valdmere had fought valiantly only to be defeated in the end. Against overpowering odds, they had come close to victory and it had been snatched from them. In a few more minutes Professor Valdmere's secret would be in the hands of the conspirators.

Despairing, weary in mind and body, Ted slumped back against the wall, his unseeing eyes fixed upon the now familiar surroundings of the room. Brooding there over the hopelessness of the outcome he could see now how puny had been his own efforts, with what vaunting egotism he had set out to pit his meager strength and cunning against a force so patently more powerful. With what secret contempt the conspirators must have looked upon him. He had been outwitted, outflanked, made to play a fool's part from the very beginning. The thought stung his pride and slowly aroused a deep-seated and wholly uncontrollable anger. Unconsciously he bit his lips, striving to keep back the hot tears of vexation and despair that would persist in coming unbidden to his staring, bloodshot eyes.

Then, quite unexpectedly, something within him seemed to snap. A sudden mad desire to risk all in one last, desperate attempt. A feeling of recklessness, an urge beyond his control, a mounting fury that scorned even such overpowering odds. Once more he stood erect, the weight of his body thrown forward on the balls of his feet, muscles tightening and every sense alert.

Barely five feet away stood the man who had taken over the reins of authority during the absence of Miss Valdmere's captor. He was conversing with a newcomer, a well-dressed, almost distinguished-looking man who had just entered the hotel. Though others of the gang had not relaxed their vigilance, it was very apparent that the leader had. He paid no more attention to Ted and Philo than if they had been two sticks of office furniture. His face was turned in profile and there was a sort of absorbtion about his manner that precluded any doubt whatsoever that his sole attention centered anywhere except around the person with whom he talked.

His mind working swiftly, Ted's eyes guaged the distance that separated them. Moistening his dry lips, he shot a meaning glance toward Philo, winking furtively. Then his gaze returned, focussing upon the bulge in the man's right hip pocket. Without a word of warning, even to his chum, he suddenly crouched low and sprang into the air.

He landed exactly where he had planned, neither
an inch to the right nor to the left—exactly and
precisely behind the broad figure of his unsuspect-
ing victim. Swaying only a split-second to keep
his balance, his hand darted forward with the quick-
ness of light and came back as swiftly, frenziedly
grasping the gun. Its cold, murderous nozzle mas-
saged the stalwart back which formed a human
screen between him and the five other conspirators.
He heard his own voice, sharp and querulous, ringing out through the startled silence.

"If any of you crooks make one move, I'll pull this
trigger. Philo, come here."

His chum's frantic scrambling to this new point
of vantage did him credit. Two figures instead of
one were now hiding behind the human screen. But
the revolver had been removed from the region of
the man's back and now pointed menacingly straight
at the surprised quintette.

"Beginning with the man on the left," Ted commanded, "step forward and let me take your weapons.
I'm desperate. I'll shoot every one of you if necessary. Keep your hands up. Now step lively please."

Outwitted at last, there was really nothing the
huddled group could do but obey. One at a time
they came forward, and one at a time, their revolvers
were removed from concealing pockets and added
to the collection Philo was deftly distributing about

his person. This accomplished, Ted called out to the white-faced clerk behind the counter:

"Call up the sheriff's office and the town's police and tell them to come down here right away. Everybody else please stand still. I mean it when I say I'll shoot the first person who tries to get out of this room. No confusion and no talking! Philo, slip over and watch the front door while I remain here to prevent any attempt to escape into the dining room."

Thereafter for a time, the voice of the clerk complying with Ted's instructions, was the only sound that smote across the room. After that the silence dropped again like a curtain. Tense and breathless, crooks, hotel guests and the two boys passed through an inervating nerve-jangling period of waiting. Presently various minor sounds came out of the death-like quiet. Here and there a man coughed or cleared his throat. Now and again a foot shuffled. Then a party of four persons, presumably hotel guests, advanced up the stone steps to the front door from the street and were promptly warned away by the door's grim, white-faced guardian. And in the end, when patience and endurance seemed no longer possible, Philo's excited voice:

"Miss Valdmere and the man coming! Ted! Ted!"

Here was an unthought of contingency.

"Hold him—hold him if you can!" shouted Ted.

Right then the revolver roared in Philo's hand, shaking the glass in the windows. A girl screamed. Still keeping the crooks covered, Ted darted across the room. From out of the corner of one eye, he saw Miss Valdmere half-swaying near the foot of the stone steps and, further along the street, a man racing and dodging through the crowds, a bulky package clutched tightly under his arm. A transitory glimpse, yet it was enough to tell him that the conspirator had escaped. Again his gaze swept the room. The seven men had not moved. Behind the counter the hotel clerk stood, white and immobile as a carven statue. Little eddies of smoke drifted in through the door and floated across the room. Then figures were darting up the stone steps. A heavy voice boomed out:

"I'm the deputy sheriff. What's wrong here?"

CHAPTER XXIX.

FATHER AND DAUGHTER

No sooner had the deputy-sheriff and his party taken charge of Ted's prisoners than the two boys were out of the door and down the stone steps. In the next instant they had surrounded Miss Valdmere. The same thoughts were uppermost in their minds, the same question trembled on their lips. Ted caught the girl's arms and stared eagerly in her face.

"Tell us—tell us, Miss Peggy. Did he—did he——"

His breath caught and his voice dwindled to a rasping unintelligent murmur. He was sure that he had read in her look what she, in her disappointment, hesitated to impart. Then he dropped her arms and stepped back, staggered by the change that had miraculously come over her.

For Miss Valdmere was radiant. Her face flashed a glorious smile. Tears of real joy coursed down her cheeks..

"Philo—Ted," she murmured happily, "I'm glad

I can inform you that—that Mr. Evanson arrived in time. We've won!"

Ted stood as one transfixed. Dazedly Philo put up one hand to his head, crying out in wonder. A crowd gathered around them. Dust from many feet, from the line of vehicular traffic moving slowly along Brownsville's principal thoroughfare, uprose and floated like a canopy above their heads, while everywhere across prairie and town streamed bright shafts of golden sunlight.

Gaping crowds. Staring, curious eyes. Bustle—confusion. Yet entirely oblivious of it all, the three stood, a tiny island in the living, human stream eddying around them.

"I knew we had won even before I entered the bank," Miss Valdmere was saying. "You see, I met Mr. Evanson coming out. When he passed me there was a smile on his face."

"You mean to say," Ted's voice sounded incredulous, "that the conspirator didn't even recognize him."

"No, that's the glorious part of it," she replied. "It was the one weak spot in their armor. I'm sure now that when we landed in Brownsville this morning no one witnessed our arrival."

"So our plans didn't miscarry after all," enthused Ted. "Everything didn't work out just as we had

suspected, but the result is just the same. We outwitted the crooks. They got the false papers."

Unexpectedly Philo drew in his breath eagerly
and pointed away through the crowd.

"Look, Miss Valdmere! Look, Ted! There he
is now."

"Who?"

"Mr. Evanson."

And Mr. Evanson it proved to be. He joined
them a moment later, grinning as he came up. Immediately all three surrounded him, plying him with
questions. Ted himself thumped him on the back.

"Mr. Evanson," he laughed, "I guess you're the
only one of us who can truthfully say that he carried
out his instructions to the letter. How did you
manage to do it?"

"Well, you see," the other answered modestly, "I
can't take very much credit myself. It was your
plan to begin with, Ted, and we have a wonderful
ally in Sheriff Warner. I doubt if any of the crooks
will escape."

"Where is the sheriff now?" asked Philo.

Some of his men are guarding the roads leading
out of the village," Mr. Evanson explained. "But
the sheriff has hurried over to the professor's estate
with a small party of determined men, whom he re-
cruited from among his own friends here in Brownsville. The reason he went to the estate is because

he wanted to make sure that nothing happened to your father, Miss Valdmere. I am positive that he has handled the situation capably and that Professor Valdmere is a free man right now. Sheriff Warner believes that one of the arch-crooks is this man Bernard, the private secretary. He is very anxious to capture Bernard on the place. What do you say we all go over there right away?"

"I'd like to go very much," stated Ted.

"So would I," said Philo.

Mr. Evanson laughed and turned upon the girl.

"And you, Miss Valdmere, I don't suppose you'd care to accompany us?"

"Oh indeed not!" she smiled back at him.

"And we couldn't possibly persuade you to come?" he persisted.

"Well, you might try," she laughed. "On second thought, exercising a young lady's prerogative, I believe I will listen to reason."

"We're so glad," said Mr. Evanson, continuing with his joking.

"If you want the truth," Miss Valdmere's voice had a determined ring to it, "wild horses couldn't pull me away. I'd go there if I had to crawl every foot of the way on my hands and knees. Father is there and I propose to see him."

Mr. Evanson smiled again and patted the shoulder of the eager girl.

"Very well then, all of you follow me. A short distance down the street a car is waiting for us."

Though Professor's Valdmere's estate was only a short distance from the center of the town, it took them much longer to get there than they had expected. The reason for this was that crowds were so dense that they clogged the sidewalks and overflowed the streets, much to the sorrow and vexation of the impatient motorist. Then, too, automobiles were almost as thick as people and, despite every effort on the part of the volunteer traffic police, nearly all of the principal thoroughfares were congested tangles, almost defying solution. Long before the little party of four had reached the gates of the professor's estate, its patience was worn to a shred.

"And to think," gasped Ted, "that all these folks expect to witness the demonstration! It's a good thing they knew nothing of what was going on behind the scenes. They actually believed those stories published in the papers. As far as they know, Professor Valdmere has been surrounded by friends all this while. It seems incredible!"

The gate at last! A word from Mr. Evanson to the guard and they had passed safely through. Whereupon happenings crowded thick and fast. It was almost bewildering. Ted could almost believe that he was asleep, treading his way through a maze of bewildering scenes, a spectator viewing a strange and unreal drama.

The thing that left the most vivid impress upon his mind was the reunion of Miss Valdmere and her father. A gray-haired man running to meet them! A glad cry—the quick movement of someone in the seat beside him, someone that flashed out of the car and streaked, like some fluttering bird, straight within the comforting haven of two encircling arms. He heard voices that were smothered in sobs. Then they were standing arm in arm, still looking into each others eyes.

"Oh, Daddy, I'm so glad I found you."

The great Professor Valdmere withdrew his arm from hers and patted the golden head.

"We have found each other, dear. My daughter—Peggy!"

And that was all that Ted and Philo heard. Abashed, they turned away and a few minutes later they had joined Mr. Evanson, who introduced them to Sheriff Warner and his men, with whom were a number of prisoners. Among these, the sheriff pointed out one, a person in whose face was depicted more despair and emotion than the others. Ted's curiosity was arouseed.

"Who is that man?" he asked.

"That," answered the sheriff turning upon Ted with a smile, "is the traitor who sold his own soul for a mess of pottage—the most miserable and despicable crook of them all—Henry Bernard, Professor Valdmere's private secretary. If you boys will come with us, I shouldn't be surprised—in fact, I'm pretty sure that you'll hear something that will throw a little light upon this case."

"What do you mean?" puzzled Ted.

"I mean a complete confession," smiled the sheriff. "Bernard has indicated his desire to make a clean breast of this whole affair. You may hear something that will surprise you."

CHAPTER XXX.

BERNARD CONFESSES

LESS than two hours later, behind locked doors in the office of the sheriff in the county courthouse in Brownsville, Sheriff Warner fixed his gaze upon the cringing face of the man who sat just opposite.

"Now, Mr. Bernard, I believe we're ready. Mr. Evanson, Mr. Winters and Mr. Birch have been summoned here at my request to be witness to your confession. Tell us what you know about the gang of crooks and how you happened to join them."

The prisoner's thin, long hands reached forward and gripped the edge of the table.

"Well, if you want to know, they're the most powerful organization of professional criminals in the world today. Their membership includes nearly every nationality and they have agencies in every important city in three continents.

"Agents, representing their organization, approached me about a month ago. They offered me a large sum of money to assist them in obtaining the formulas for Professor Valdmere's Atomic Ray.

I refused, but they kept persisting, kept hounding me, offering greater and greater rewards, until finally I agreed to their demands."

"What did they want you to do?" asked the sheriff.

"My orders were to buy off all the guards and other employees working upon the estate. I discharged many of the old guards, and hired new ones—crooks—to take their places.

"It was arranged that the theft of the formulas for the Atomic Ray should take place on Sunday evening, June 23rd, just one day before he was to give his demonstration. Then Miss Valdmere wrote that she would arrive in Brownsville on Saturday, June 22nd. That meant that she would be with her father on the night set for the theft of the Atomic Ray. For a while I did not know how I was to meet this new emergency."

The sheriff raised a gnarled hand.

"Why should the girl's appearance make a great deal of difference one way or the other? Why couldn't you imprison her just as you did her father?"

The prisoner rubbed one cheek with the palm of his hand and gazed thoughtfully out of the window.

"I couldn't bring myself to subject Miss Valdmere to such a horrible ordeal."

"Why was it so horrible?" the sheriff persisted.

"Because members of the organization proposed to murder Professor Valdmere just as soon as they gained possession of the secret of the Atomic Ray. The organization had already entered into an agreement with representatives of a foreign government to deliver the secret intact. The crooks had to make sure the secret was theirs and theirs alone before they could collect the stupendous sum agreed upon. This was impossible as long as Professor Valdmere lived. I felt it was my duty to shield Miss Valdmere—and shield her I did."

"How?"

"As soon as I learned that she was coming to Brownsville, I went to a man who is at the head of the organization and insisted that in some way we must induce the girl to leave the estate. I told him that I couldn't endure the thought of having her there, and unless he could devise some means of taking her out of sight of all the terrible things about to happen, I would refuse to carry out my end of the agreement.

"The plan ultimately agreed upon did not entirely meet with my approval but I was forced to accept it. You are familiar with the plan so I need not go into details concerning it."

"I'm not so sure about that," objected Sheriff Warner. "It isn't as clear to us as you might suppose. There is a question or two I'd like to ask you.   First of all, was it your intention to lead Miss Valdmere to believe that her father had been captured by enemies and taken to Langdon Prairie?"

"Yes."

"How did you contrive to do that?"

"Before we broke open Professor Valdmere's safe to examine its contents, we wrote a note and left it on the floor in the office. We were sure that she would find it the moment she entered to look for her father."

"Why couldn't Miss Valdmere find her father before she left the estate. According to these young men here she did not find the note until after she had made a thorough search of the premises. Where did you have him concealed?"

"On the night before Miss Valdmere's arrival, three of the guards and myself cut a hole in the floor of the work-shop and made a small excavation in the earth underneath. Professor Valdmere was bound and gagged and thrust into that hole."

"These young men also claim that one of your men posed as Professor Valdmere. Why was it necessary to practice such a deception?"

"The reason is obvious. We felt that the note alone might not in itself be sufficent. We wanted to be sure that after she had reached Langdon Prairie she would continue to follow the automobile in which she believed her father was held captive."

"But weren't you aware that when Miss Valdmere was brought face to face with the imposter she would recognize the duplicity?"

"Certainly we were aware of it," Bernard replied. "On the other hand, we knew that from a short distance away she would be unable to tell whether the man was an imposter or not."

"What was your idea in luring Miss Valdmere to the hills?" came the next question.

"It is an unfrequented region where our party would be fairly safe. It was our intention to hold Miss Valdmere there until I could join her."

"Then what did you propose to do?"

"Take her with me to the place where I was going."

"Where were you going?"

"Asia or South America—I hadn't quite decided."

"Were you in constant communication with your party which was decoying Miss Valdmere?"

"Yes."

"How did you manage this?"

"They carried a small radio-telephone equipment with them."

CHAPTER XXXI.

THE PLOT UNFOLDS

SHERIFF WARNER flecked the ash from his cigar, fumbled in his pockets for a match, scowled, then, with a gesture of disgust, tossed the half-smoked stub into a nearby waste paper basket. After that he glowered at the prisoner, at the same time pulling at the short, bristling ends of his moustache.

"A peculiar case," he mused. "An extraordinary case! Now, Mr. Bernard, I wish you would tell us why, after sending the girl away, you wanted to get her back. I think I know why myself but I want you to confirm my opinion."

"It all centers around the formulas for the Atomic Ray," the prisoner told him. "Up until the evening of June 23rd, when we blew open the safe in Professor Valdmere's office, we had been certain that we would find the secret there. I knew that my employer kept all his valuable papers in that safe and that he alone had the combination. We were dumbfounded, therefore, after blowing it open, to discover that the formulas were not there. It was not

until late in the afternoon of the next day that I
suddenly recalled that Miss Valdmere had taken a
parcel to the bank, placing it in a safety-deposit box.
I had accompanied Miss Valdmere at the time—it
was on Saturday afternoon, June 22nd."

"Why were you so sure that those were the papers
you wanted, the formulas, I mean?"

"We weren't sure, of course," Bernard smiled a
wan smile. "Nevertheless, we were quite sure."

"Please explain yourself."

"Follow a natural course of reasoning and you
will arrive at that deduction yourself. We had not
overlooked any possible hiding place on the estate.
I have charge of all Professor Valdmere's corre-
spondence, his letters, express parcels—everything of
that sort. I do all his ordering for machinery parts,
chemicals, laboratory equipment, and so forth. Since
coming to Brownsville the professor had left the
estate only twice and on both occasions I had accompanied him. Now it stood to reason that those
formulas couldn't have disappeared into thin air.
By a process of elimination, we deduced that the only
way they could have been taken away from the
estate was through the agency of Miss Valdmere;
and, inasmuch as Miss Valdmere had left the estate
only once since her arrival, on that Saturday afternoon when she went to the bank with the parcel,
we were quite sure the formulas must be there."

"Yes, yes, go on."

"So, having come to that conclusion, we immediately began to lay our plans to get them. As you can see for yourself, two courses were open to us. The first was to induce Miss Valdmere to obtain them for us, and the other was to force an entrance into the bank and endeavor to steal them. We decided that obtaining them through the medium of Miss Valdmere would be our safest plan. Failing in that, we could resort to the second alternative."

The prisoner paused. "Everything quite clear?" he asked.

"Perfectly."

"Very well, then, I'll proceed. Our first act was to get in touch with our party in the hills and inquire if Miss Valdmere was with them. She wasn't. It was known, however, that she had left Langdon Prairie in an automobile in company with a young man and was on her way there."

Ted suddenly sat up straight, gripping the sides of his chair.

"How did the party in the hills know that?" he demanded.

"Because our confederates up there were not only in communication with us but were also in communication with one of our agents in Langdon Prairie."

"Then what did you do?" asked the sheriff.

"Upon ascertaining that another young man, pre-

viously one of Miss Valdmere's companions, had
been captured and was at that moment with our party
in the hills, we gave instructions that he should be
permitted to escape, taking a message to Miss Valdmere, purporting to come from her father. The
message must instruct the girl to return immediately
to Brownsville and remove the papers from the
bank. When she did that, our intention, of course,
was to seize both the papers and Miss Valdmere."

"When Miss Valdmere arrived in Brownsville
this morning, did you think that she had come to follow out those instructions?"

"No, on the contrary, we were sure that she
wouldn't. A number of things had happened in the
meantime to lead us to believe that the real motive
for Miss Valdmere's return was to find her father.
Our reason for thinking so was based upon information we had received from the leader of the hills'
party. For example, at two o'clock yesterday afternoon we learned that our man, impersonating Professor Valdmere, had been forcibly taken from our
camp by two persons, one of whom was the young
man we had previously permitted to escape. Six
hours later we received another message to the effect that the impersonator, having succeeded in al-
luding his two captors, had returned to camp bearing the startling news that he had met Miss Vald-

mere face to face and that she had penetrated his disguise.

"Upon learning this, we ordered the entire party to advance to the place where Miss Valdmere had been seen by the impersonator, capture her and bring her to Brownsville as quickly as possible. This morning we were anxiously awaiting word from them, when, to our great astonishment, one of our men encountered the girl and her two companions here on the main street of Brownsville."

"So you immediately laid your trap for her?"

"Naturally."

"Is it true"—Sheriff Warner glared at his prisoner —"that you proposed to live up to your agreement made with the girl to spare Professor Valdmere's life if she went to the bank and secured the formulas?"

"No," Bernard shook his head, "as I have already explained to you, that would have been impossible."

"And you had no intention to make good your promise?"

"No."

"You would have murdered him just the same?"

"Yes."

Sheriff Warner bit his lower lip and turned thoughtfully upon Ted and Philo.

"Are there any questions either one of you would like to ask the prisoner?" he inquired.

Philo shook his head. "I don't think there are,"
he replied. "What about you, Ted?"

Ted slid forward in his seat eagerly.

"Yes, there are a number of things which are not
yet quite clear to me. So far in his confession Mr.
Bernard has made no mention of the three Russians
we encountered first at Langdon Prairie and afterward up in the hills. Were these men also members
of your organization?" he inquired of the prisoner.

"No, they were not," Bernard informed them.
"Like ourselves, they, too, hoped to gain possession
of the secret. The first intimation we had of their
existence was when our car, conveying the impersonator to Langdon Prairie, was traced to that town
by those three crooks. No doubt they had been
watching us for several days. They must have seen
the imposter in the car when our party drove through
Brownsville on its way to Langdon Prairie and immediately jumped to the conclusion that the impersonator was the real Professor Valdmere. Our men
had a little trouble in eluding them at Langdon,"
he smiled. "The desire to be rid of them caused us
to commit a slight imprudence."

"What was it?" asked the sheriff.

"On one occasion our car was being followed by
a young man in another car. We suspected that he
was one of the Russians and resorted to a certain
trick in an effort to throw him off our trail."

"I am that young man," grinned Ted. "One of the Japs in your party approached the constable of Langdon Prairie and pretended that they were trying to find Professor Valdmere."

"Yes, that is correct. We were not aware of our mistake until our agent in Langdon Prairie reported that you were one of Miss Valdmere's escorts and were following the imposter to the hills."

"What I can't understand," Ted scratched his head, "is why you didn't capture Miss Valdmere at the same time you captured my friend Mr. Birch."

"For two reasons," explained Bernard. "At the time we seized your friend Miss Valdmere's first act was to turn and start to run. If we had followed her, she might have gone screaming into one the houses in that neighborhood, causing a good deal of unnecessary stir. Soon the police would have been on our trail."

"And the other reason?"

"We were sure that she would follow us. We were in no particular hurry to take her anyway until our party had arrived in the hills."

"Any other questions?" The sheriff looked at Ted.

"No, Mr. Warner, I can't think of any."

They were preparing to rise when a telephone bell jangled loudly. Leaning forward, the sheriff snatched up the instrument on his desk and barked into it. An interval of silence, then:

"Well! Well! Well" he exclaimed excitedly.

Fearing some new development in the case, Ted leaped to his feet.

"What is it?" he demanded.

Sheriff Warner placed one large hand over the mouthpiece and turned his beaming face toward the two boys.

"Good news!" he shouted. "The ranchers' posse has just arrived at Stebbing's with its convoy of Japanese and Russian prisoners. Setting out for Brownsville this afternoon!"

CHAPTER XXXII

THE ATOMIC RAY

THAT same afternoon Ted and Philo were amongst the crowd that poured through the gate onto Professor Valdmere's estate. Like a huge, dark tide the moving throngs spread out, covering the grassy, level field to the east of the set of low buildings where an immense platform had been raised and upon which surrounded by instruments, screens and queer-looking mechanical devices, Professor Valdmere was getting ready to give his long-delayed first public demonstration of the Atomic Ray.

Moving toward the front of the platform a few minutes later, the great scientist suddenly raised one arm, commanding silence.

"Ladies and gentlemen," he began, "because of the short time I have at my disposal, I will not be given an opportunity to apologize as fully as I would wish for the regrettable delay in keeping my——"

He got no further. An enthusiastic burst of applause swept up and down the field, culminating in wild and vociferous cheering.

"No need for apologies! Let's have the demonstration! Show us the Atomic Ray! To blazes with the crooks!" shrill voices shouted on every hand.

Professor Valdmere smiled, bowed, made a gesture to indicate that he understood, and stepped back to a small table upon which was a single earthen jar.

Thrusting his hand in the jar, he brought out what appeared to be an ordinary chunk of metal. Again he signalled for silence.

"In order to make clear to everyone what I am about to do, it will be necessary to give you a brief synopsis of the more recent findings of science in the field of atomic energy."

In a clear, steady voice, the professor went on to describe the character and compositions of atoms. He spoke of the mysterious, dynamic force lurking in these tiny microscopic bodies and of the electrons that separated from them, volleying out into space at terrific, unbelievable speed to form electro-magnetic streams, which, when converted to the uses of mankind, would provide unlimited heat and power for all time to come.

Concluding his explanations, Professor Valdmere strode to the back of the platform, placed the chunk of metal in a container resting upon a curious-looking mechanical contrivance that stood near a large chemical screen, then touched a button near his hand. Instantly a dazzling flame of tremendous

intensity flashed from the screen and spread out in
every direction until it had mantled the earth for
rods around in a magic purple twilight. A finger
moved toward the button again and it was gone.
Smiling, the scientist walked to the edge of the platform and looked down into the awed faces upturned
to his.

"What you have just witnessed," he explained,
"is no miraculous manifestation when considered
in the light of our new scientific knowledge. The
purple light spreading from my chemical screen
is nothing more or less than energetic particles,
which we call electrons, checked in their flight
through space and made visible to the human eye.
The electrons producing that light all came from the
small lump of metal which I held in my hand a few
moments ago and afterward placed in the container
attached to the device I have perfected for stimu-
lating radio-activity in all forms of matter.

"I can increase or decrease the intensity of this
Atomic Ray at will. Increasing it, if I dared, I
would have a flame of energy so powerful that life
itself would wither before it. Here is the force
that will drive the wheels of industry tomorrow
and for all time. This Atomic Ray is no invention
of mine, no chance discovery of the moment. Even
before the dawn of civilization it has been lashing
its comet-like way through Nature's mighty store-

room, waiting for the ingenuity of man to turn it to account."

When Professor Valdmere had completed his demonstration, Ted and Philo, still gaping after the manner of two small children, swung about and thoughtfully followed the crowd surging back in the direction of the gate. Almost there, a young lady, wearing a pretty new dress and a rose pinned in her hair, stepped out in front of them, effectively barring their way.

"Am I to understand," she inquired in an injured voice, "that you two young miscreants really intended to get away from here without saying good-bye?"

"Why, no, Miss Peggy—why, no. You—see ——" Ted's voice faltered and his eyes sought the ground.

"We were only walking toward the gate," stated Philo quite stupidly.

The girl's eyes twinkled.

"Going back to your hotel, I suppose, and afterward boarding your train for home."

"Pretty much what we had planned," Ted admitted, "except for one thing. We would have telephoned you."

"Well, I like that," Miss Valdmere pouted. "One would think that we were only casual acquaintances instead of—instead of——"

. "Being friends for two whole long days," Philo completed the sentence for her.

They all laughed heartily at this merry quip, whereupon Miss Valdmere again became serious.

"Dad can hardly wait to see you. Both of you are going up to the house this very minute. There is an important matter to be discussed and settled before another day comes around."

"What is this matter?" wondered Philo.

"I'm not supposed to tell you," Miss Valdmere's manner was mysterious.

"I'll bet I know," guessed Philo. "He wants to know what Bernard told us this afternoon at the court house."

"Wrong," said Miss Valdmere. "He's more anxious to know what two young men will say when he offers them a life-long partnership in a new firm to be known as Valdmere and Associates."

Ted began to tremble from head to foot.

"Eh wh—what—" he stammered.

"I'm the Valdmere and you two are the Associates."

"You're spoofing!" cried Ted.

"Not a bit of it!" Miss Valdmere scorned the accusation. "I was never more serious in my life. It's to be a real firm."

"What kind of a firm?" asked Philo.

Miss Valdmere laughed.

"A manufacturing firm, I think."

"A manufacturing firm!" stared Ted. "What are we going to make?"

The girl did not hesitate.

"We're going to make provisions for the future, plans to protect Father, new and clever devices for catching crooks."

Miss Valdmere paused, brushed back a wisp of golden hair and smiled at the senior Associate.

"Yes, yes, Miss Peggy."

"And, O, Ted——"

"Another thing—something I've wanted to do all my life—you're going to teach me how to fly."

THE END.